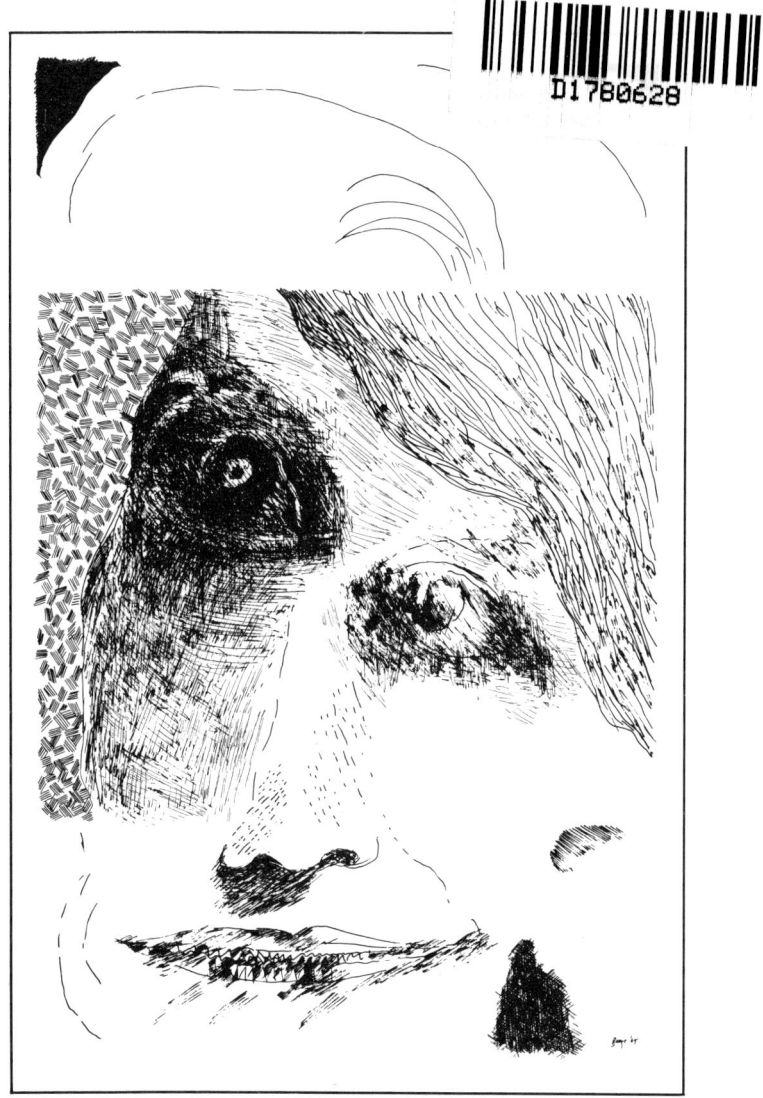

GOD IS NOT A FISH INSPECTOR
W. D. VALGARDSON

PS
8593
A45
G6

ALGOMA COLLEGE LIBRARY

AN OBERON BOOK

GOD IS NOT A FISH INSPECTOR

Although Emma made no noise as she descended, Fusi Bergman knew his daughter was watching him from the bottom of the stairs.

"God will punish you," she promised in a low, intense voice.

"Render unto Caesar what is Caesar's," he snapped. "God's not a fish inspector. He doesn't work for the government."

By the light of the front ring of the kitchen stove, he had been drinking a cup of coffee mixed half and half with whisky. Now, he shifted in his captain's chair so as to partly face the stairs. Though he was unable to make out more than the white blur of Emma's nightgown, after living with her for 48 years he knew exactly how she would look if he turned on the light.

She was tall and big boned with the square, pugnacious face of a bulldog. Every inch of her head would be crammed with metal curlers and her angular body hidden by a plain white cotton shift that hung from her broad shoulders like a tent. Whenever she was angry with him, she always stood rigid and white lipped, her hands clenched at her sides.

"You prevaricate," she warned. "You will not be able to prevaricate at the gates of Heaven."

He drained his cup, sighed, and pulled on his jacket. As he opened the door, Fusi said, "He made fish to catch. There is no place in the Bible where it says you can't catch fish when you are three score and ten."

"You'll be the ruin of us," she hissed as he closed the door on her.

She was aggressive and overbearing, but he knew her too well to be impressed. Behind her forcefulness, there was always that trace of self-pity nurtured in plain women who go unmarried until they think they have been passed by. Even if they eventually found a husband, the self-pity returned to change their determination into a whine. Still, he was glad to have the door between them.

This morning, as every morning, he had wakened at three. Years before, he had trained himself to get up at that time and now, in spite of his age, he never woke more than five minutes after the hour. He was proud of his early rising for he felt it showed he was not, like many of his contemporaries, relentlessly sliding into the endless blur of senility. Each morning, because he had become reconciled to the idea of dying, he felt, on the instant of his awakening, a spontaneous sense of amazement at being alive. The thought never lasted longer than the brief time between sleep and consciousness, but the good feeling lingered throughout the day.

When Fusi stepped outside, the air was cold and damp. The moon that hung low in the west was pale and fragile and very small. 50 feet from the house, the breakwater that ran along the rear of his property loomed like the purple spine of some great beast guarding the land from a lake which seemed, in the darkness, to go on forever.

Holding his breath to still the noise of his own breathing, Fusi listened for a cough or the scuff of gravel that would mean someone was close by, watching and waiting, but the only sound was the muted rubbing of his skiff against the piling to which it was moored. Half a mile away where the land was lower, rows of gas boats roped five abreast lined the docks. The short, stubby boats with their high cabins, the grey surface of the docks and the dark water were all tinged purple from the mercury lamps. At the harbour mouth, high on a thin spire, a red light burned like a distant star.

Behind him, he heard the door open and, for a moment, he was afraid Emma might begin to shout, or worse still, turn on the back-door light and alert his enemies, but she did neither. Above all things, Emma was afraid of scandal, and would do anything to avoid causing an unsavoury rumour to be attached to her own or her husband's name.

Her husband, John Smith, was as bland and inconsequential as his name. Moon faced with wide blue eyes and a small mouth above which sat a carefully trimmed moustache, he was a head shorter than Emma and a good 50 pounds lighter. Six years before, he had been transferred to the Eddyville branch of the Bank of Montreal. His transfer from Calgary to a small town in Manitoba was the bank's way of letting him know that there would be no more promotions. He would stay in Eddyville until he retired.

A year after he arrived, Emma had married him and instead of her moving out, he had moved in. For the last two years, under Emma's prodding, John had been taking a correspondence course in theology so that when he no longer worked at the bank he could be a full-time preacher.

On the evenings when he wasn't balancing the bank's books, he laboured over the multiple-choice questions in the Famous Preacher's course that he received each month from the One True and Only Word of God Church in Mobile, Alabama. Because of a freak in the atmosphere one night while she had been fiddling with the radio, Emma had heard a gospel hour advertising the course and, although neither she nor John had ever been south of Minneapolis and had never heard of the One True and Only Word of God Church before, she took it as a sign and immediately enrolled her husband in it. It cost $500.

John's notes urged him not to wait to answer His Call but to begin ministering to the needy at once for the Judgment Day was always imminent. In anticipation of the end of the world and his need for a congregation once he retired, he and Emma had become zealous missionaries, cramming their Volkswagen with a movie projector, a record-player, films, trays of slides, religious records for every occasion, posters and pamphlets, all bought or rented from the One True and Only Word of God Church. Since the townspeople were obstinately Lutheran, and since John did not want to give offence to any of his bank's customers, he and Emma hunted converts along the grey dirt roads that led past tumble-down farmhouses, the inhabitants of which were never likely to enter a bank.

Fusi did not turn to face his daughter but hurried away because he knew he had no more than an hour and a half until dawn. His legs were fine as he crossed the yard, but by the time he had mounted the steps that led over the breakwater, then climbed down fifteen feet to the shore, his left knee had begun to throb.

Holding his leg rigid to ease the pain, he waded out, loosened the ropes and heaved himself away from the shore. As soon as the boat was in deep water, he took his seat, and set both oars in the oar-locks he had carefully muffled with strips from an old shirt.

For a moment, he rested his hands on his knees, the oars rising like too-small wings from a cumbersome body, then he straightened his arms, dipped the oars cleanly into the water and in one smooth motion pulled his hands toward his chest. The first few strokes were even and graceful but then as a speck of pain like a grain of sand formed in his shoulder, the sweep of his left oar became shorter than his right. Each time he leaned against the oars, the pain grew until it was, in his mind, a bent shingle-nail twisted and turned in his shoulder socket.

With the exertion, a ball of gas formed in his stomach, making him uncomfortable. As quickly as a balloon being blown up, it expanded until his lungs and heart were cramped and he couldn't draw in a full breath. Although the air over the lake was cool, sweat ran from his hairline.

At his two-hundredth stroke, he shipped his left oar and pulled a coil of rope with a large hook from under the seat.

After checking to see that it was securely tied through the gunwale, he dropped the rope overboard and once more began to row. Normally, he would have had a buoy made from a slender tamarack pole, a block of wood and some lead weights to mark his net, but he no longer had a fishing licence so his net had to be sunk below the surface where it could not be seen by the fish inspectors.

Five more strokes of the oars and the rope went taut. He lifted both oars into the skiff, then, standing in the bow, began to pull. The boat responded sluggishly but gradually it turned and the cork line that lay hidden under two feet of water broke the surface. He grasped the net, freed the hook and began to collect the mesh until the lead line appeared. For once he had been lucky and the hook had caught the net close to one end so there was no need to backtrack.

Hand over hand he pulled, being careful not to let the corks and leads bang against the bow, for on the open water sound carried clearly for miles. In the first two fathoms there was a freshly caught pickerel. As he pulled it toward him, it beat the water with its tail, making light, slapping sounds. His fingers were cramped, but Fusi managed to catch the fish around its soft middle and, with his other hand, work the mesh free of the gills.

It was then that the pain in his knee forced him to sit. Working from the seat was awkward and cost him precious time, but he had no choice, for the pain had begun to inch up the bone toward his crotch.

He wiped his forehead with his hand and cursed his infirmity. When he was twenty, he had thought nothing of rowing five miles from shore to lift five and six gangs of nets and then, nearly knee deep in fish, row home again. Now, he reflected bitterly, a quarter of a mile and one net were nearly beyond him. Externally, he had changed very little over the years. He was still tall and thin, his arms and legs corded with muscle. His belly was hard. His long face, with its pointed jaw, showed his age the most. That and his hands. His face was lined until it seemed there was nowhere the skin was smooth. His hands were scarred and heavily veined. His hair was grey but it was still thick.

While others were amazed at his condition, he was afraid of the changes that had taken place inside him. It was this invisible deterioration that was gradually shrinking the limits of his endurance.

Even in the darkness, he could see the distant steeple of the Lutheran church and the square bulk of the old folk's home that was directly across from his house. Emma, he thought grimly, would not be satisfied until he was safely trapped in one or carried out of the other.

He hated the old folk's home. He hated the three stories of pale yellow brick with their small, close-set windows. He hated the concrete porch with its five round pillars and the large white buckets of red geraniums. When he saw the men poking at the flowers like a bunch of old women, he pulled his blinds.

The local people who worked in the home were good to the inmates, tenants they called them, but there was no way a man could be a man in there. No whisky. Going to bed at ten. Getting up at eight. Bells for breakfast, coffee and dinner. Bells for everything. He was surprised that they didn't have bells for going to the toilet. Someone watching over you every minute of every day. It was as if, having earned the right to be an adult, you had suddenly, in some inexplicable way, lost it again.

The porch was the worst part of the building. Long and narrow and lined with yellow and red rocking-chairs, it sat ten feet above the ground and the steps were so steep that even those who could get around all right were afraid to try them. Fusi had lived across from the old folk's home for 40 years and he had seen old people, all interchangeable as time erased their identities, shuffling and bickering their way to their deaths. Now, most of those who came out to sleep in the sun and to watch the world with glittering, jealous eyes, were people he had known.

He would have none of it. He was not afraid of dying, but

he was determined that it would be in his own home. His licence had been taken from him because of his age, but he did not stop. One net was not thirty, but it was one, and a quarter-mile from shore was not five miles, but it was a quarter-mile.

He didn't shuffle and he didn't have to be fed or have a rubber diaper pinned around him each day. If anything, he had become more cunning for, time and again, the inspectors had come and destroyed the illegal nets of other fishermen, even catching and sending them to court to be fined, but they hadn't caught him for four years. Every day of the fishing season, he pitted his wits against theirs and won. At times, they had come close, but their searches had never turned up anything and, once, to his delight, when he was on the verge of being found with freshly caught fish on him, he hid them under a hole in the breakwater and then sat on the edge of the boat, talked about old times, and shared the inspectors' coffee. The memory still brought back a feeling of pleasure and excitement.

As his mind strayed over past events, he drew the boat along the net in fits and starts for his shoulder would not take the strain of steady pulling. Another good-sized fish hung limp as he pulled it to him, but then as he slipped the mesh from its head, it gave a violent shake and flew from his hands. Too stiff and slow to lunge for it, he could do nothing but watch the white flash of its belly before it struck the water and disappeared.

He paused to knead the backs of his hands, then began again. Before he was finished, his breath roared in his ears like the lake in a storm, but there were four more pickerel. With a sigh that was nearly a cry of pain, he let the net drop. Immediately, pulled down by the heavy, rusted anchors at each end, it disappeared. People were like that, he thought. One moment they were here, then they were gone and it was as if they had never been.

Behind the town, the horizon was a pale, hard grey. The silhouette of rooftops and trees might have been cut from a child's purple construction paper.

The urgent need to reach the shore before the sky became any lighter drove Fusi, for he knew that if the inspectors saw him on the water they would catch him as easily as a child. They would take his fish and net, which he did not really mind, for there were more fish in the lake and more nets in his shed, but he couldn't afford to lose his boat. His savings were not enough to buy another.

He put out the oars, only to be unable to close the fingers of his left hand. When he tried to bend his fingers around the handle, his whole arm began to tremble. Unable to do anything else, he leaned forward and pressing his fingers flat to the seat, he began to relentlessly knead them. Alternately, he prayed and cursed, trying with words to delay the sun.

"A few minutes," he whispered through clenched teeth. "Just a few minutes more." But even as he watched, the horizon turned red, then yellow and a sliver of the sun's rim rose above the houses.

Unable to wait any longer, he grabbed his left hand in his right and forced his fingers around the oar, then braced himself and began to row. Instead of cutting the water cleanly, the left oar skimmed over the surface, twisting the handle in his grip. He tried again, not letting either oar go deep. The skiff moved sluggishly ahead.

Once again, the balloon in his chest swelled and threatened to gag him, making his gorge rise, but he did not dare stop. Again and again, the left oar skipped across the surface so that the bow swung back and forth like a wounded and dying animal trying to shake away its pain. Behind him, the orange sun inched above the sharp angles of the roofs.

When the bow slid across the sand, he dropped the oars, letting them trail in the water. He grasped the gunwale, but as he climbed out, his left leg collapsed and he slid to his knees. Cold water filled his boots and soaked the legs of his trousers. Resting his head against the boat, he breathed noisily through his mouth. He remained there until gradually his breathing eased and the pain in his chest closed like a night flower touched by daylight. When he could stand, he tied the boat to one of the black pilings that was left from a breakwater that had long since been smashed and carried away.

As he collected his catch, he noticed the green fisheries department truck on the dock. He had been right. They were there. Crouching behind his boat, he waited to see if anyone was watching him. It seemed like a miracle that they had not already seen him, but he knew that they had not for if they had, their launch would have raced out of the harbour and swept down upon him.

Bending close to the sand, he limped into the deep shadow at the foot of the breakwater. They might, he knew, be waiting for him at the top of the ladder, but if they were, there was nothing he could do about it. He climbed the ladder and, hearing and seeing nothing, he rested near the top so that when he climbed into sight, he wouldn't need to sit down.

No-one was in the yard. The block was empty. With a sigh of relief, he crossed to the small shed where he kept his equipment and hefted the fish onto the shelf that was nailed to one wall. He filleted his catch with care, leaving none of the translucent flesh on the back-bone or skin. Then, because they were pickerel, he scooped out the cheeks, which he set aside with the roe for his breakfast.

As he carried the offal across the backyard in a bucket, the line of gulls that gathered every morning on the breakwater broke into flight and began to circle overhead. Swinging back the bucket, he flung the guts and heads and skin into the air and the gulls darted down to snatch the red entrails and iridescent heads. In a thrumming of white and grey wings, those who hadn't caught anything descended to the sand to fight for what remained.

Relieved at being rid of the evidence of his fishing—if anyone asked where he got the fillets he would say he had bought them and the other fishermen would lie for him—

Fusi squatted and wiped his hands clean on the wet grass.

There was no sign of movement in the house. The blinds were still drawn and the high, narrow house with its steep roof and faded red-brick siding looked deserted. The yard was flat and bare except for the dead trunk of an elm, which was stripped bare of its bark and wind polished to the colour of bone.

He returned to the shed and wrapped the fillets in a sheet of brown waxed paper, then put the roe and the cheeks into the bucket. Neither Emma nor John were up when he came in and washed the bucket and his food, but as he started cooking, Emma appeared in a quilted housecoat covered with large, purple tulips. Her head was a tangle of metal.

"Are you satisfied?" she asked, her voice trembling. "I've had no sleep since you left."

Without turning from the stove, he said, "Leave. Nobody's making you stay."

Indignantly, she answered, "And who would look after you?"

He grimaced and turned over the roe so they would be golden brown on all sides. For two weeks around Christmas he had been sick with the flu and she never let him forget it.

"Honour thy father and mother that thy days may be long upon this earth."

He snorted out loud. What she really wanted to be sure of was that she got the house.

"You don't have to be like this," she said, starting to talk to him as if he was a child. "I only want you to stop because I care about you. All those people who live across the street, they don't...."

"I'm not one of them," he barked.

"You're 70 years old...."

"And I still fish," he replied angrily, cutting her off. "And I still row a boat and lift my nets. That's more than your husband can do and he's just 50." He jerked his breakfast off the stove. Because he knew it would annoy her, he began to eat out of the pan.

"I'm 70," he continued between bites, "and I beat the entire fisheries department. They catch men half my age, but they haven't caught me. Not for four years. And I fish right under their noses." He laughed with glee and laced his coffee with a finger of whisky.

Emma, her lips clamped shut and her hands clenched in fury, marched back up the stairs. In half an hour both she and John came down for their breakfast. Under Emma's glare, John cleared his throat and said, "Emma, that is we, think—" He stopped and fiddled with the knot of his tie. He always wore light grey ties and a light grey suit. "If you don't quit breaking the law, something will have to be done." He stopped and looked beseechingly at his wife, but she narrowed her eyes until little folds of flesh formed beneath them. "Perhaps something like putting you in custody so you'll be saved from yourself."

Fusi was so shocked that for once he could think of nothing to say. Encouraged by his silence, John said, "It will be for your own good."

Before either of them realized what he was up to, Fusi leaned sideways and emptied his cup into his son-in-law's lap.

The coffee was hot. John flung himself backward with a screech, but the back legs of his chair caught on a crack in the linoleum and he tipped over with a crash. In the confusion Fusi stalked upstairs.

In a moment he flung an armload of clothes down. When his daughter rushed to the bottom of the stairs, Fusi flung another armload of clothes at her.

"This is my house," he bellowed. "You're not running it yet."

Emma began grabbing clothes and laying them flat so they wouldn't wrinkle. John, both hands clenched between his legs, hobbled over to stare.

Fusi descended the stairs and they parted to let him by. At the counter, he picked up the package of fish and turning toward them, said, "I want you out of here when I get back or I'll go out on the lake and get caught and tell everyone that you put me up to it."

His fury was so great that once he was outside he had to lean against the house while a spasm of trembling swept over him. When he was composed, he rounded the corner. At one side of the old folk's home there was an enclosed fire escape that curled to the ground like a piece of intestine. He headed for the kitchen door under it.

Fusi had kept on his rubber boots, dark slacks and red turtle-neck sweater, and because he knew that behind the curtains, eyes were watching his every move, he tried to hide the stiffness in his left leg.

Although it was early, Rosie Melysyn was already at work. She always came first, never missing a day. She was a large, good natured widow with grey hair.

"How are you today, Mr. Bergman?" she asked.

"Fine," he replied. "I'm feeling great." He held out the brown paper package. "I thought some of the old people might like some fish." Although he had brought fish for the last four years, he always said the same thing.

Rosie dusted off her hands, took the package and placed it on the counter.

"I'll see someone gets it," she assured him. "Help yourself to some coffee."

As he took the pot from the stove, she asked, "No trouble with the inspectors?"

He always waited for her to ask that. He grinned delightedly, the pain of the morning already becoming a memory. "No trouble. They'll never catch me. I'm up too early. I saw them hanging about, but it didn't do them any good."

"Jimmy Henderson died last night," Rosie offered.

"Jimmy Henderson," Fusi repeated. They had been friends, but he felt no particular sense of loss. Jimmy had been in the home for three years. "I'm not surprised. He wasn't more than 68 but he had given up. You give up, you're going to die. You believe in yourself and you can keep right on going."

Rosie started mixing oatmeal and water.

"You know," he said to her broad back, "I was with Jimmy the first time he got paid. He cut four cords of wood for 60¢ and spent it all on hootch. He kept running up and down the street and flapping his arms, trying to fly. When he passed out, we hid him in the hayloft of the stable so his old man couldn't find him."

Rosie tried to imagine Jimmy Henderson attempting to fly and failed. To her, he was a bent man with a sad face who had to use a walker to get to the dining-room. What she remembered about him best was coming on him unexpectedly and finding him silently crying. He had not seen her and she had quietly backed away.

Fusi was lingering because after he left, there was a long day ahead of him. He would have the house to himself and after checking the vacated room to see that nothing of his had been taken, he would tie his boat properly, sleep for three hours, then eat lunch. In the afternoon he would make a trip to the docks to see what the inspectors were up to and collect information about their movements.

The back door opened with a swish and he felt a cool draft. Both he and Rosie turned to look. He was shocked to see that instead of it being one of the kitchen help, it was Emma. She shut the door and glanced at them both, then at the package of fish.

"What do you want?" he demanded.

"I called the inspectors," she replied, "to tell them you're not responsible for yourself. I told them about the net."

He gave a start, but then was relieved when he remembered they had to actually catch him fishing before they could take the skiff. "So what?" he asked, confident once more.

Quietly, she replied, "You don't have to worry about being caught. They've known about your fishing all along."

Suddenly frightened by her calm certainty, his voice rose as he said, "That's not true."

"They don't care," she repeated. "Inspector McKenzie

was the name of the one I talked to. He said you couldn't do any harm with one net. They've been watching you every morning just in case you should get into trouble and need help."

Emma stood there, not moving, her head tipped back, her eyes benevolent.

He turned to Rosie. "She's lying, isn't she? That's not true. They wouldn't do that?"

"Of course, she's lying," Rosie assured him.

He would have rushed outside but Emma was standing in his way. Since he could not get past her, he fled through the swinging doors that led to the dining-room.

As the doors shut, Rosie turned on Emma and said, "You shouldn't have done that." She picked up the package of fish with its carefully folded wrapping. In the artificial light, the package glowed like a piece of amber. She held it cupped in the hollows of her hands. "You had no right."

Emma seemed to grow larger and her eyes shone.

"The Lord's work be done," she said, her right hand partly raised as if she were preparing to give a benediction.

HUNTING

In his prime, Sonny Brum had been 280 pounds of muscle that angled sharply from broad, straight shoulders to a narrow waist, but years of sitting around a display room drinking coffee and eating jelly busters as he waited for customers had thickened him. The muscle had diminished but his appetite had not and a heavy roll of flesh sagged over his belt. His head was square, his skin swarthy and his nose, which was large and hooked, had been broken so many times that it was permanently bent to the left. A white scar curved like a third eyebrow in the middle of his forehead. When he walked, he did so with a hesitating limp.

If he had been older, he could have been a casualty of some foreign war, one of those who put on blue blazers and lay wreaths once a year, but he was not. His facial scars had been gathered in the vicious struggles of semi-pro football and his knee-cap had been smashed during the first game he played for the Winnipeg Blue Bombers. Although his first game as a pro had been his last, he had, on the wall of his office, a 24-by-18-inch photograph of himself in uniform with the rest of the team and he always carried a wallet-size duplicate along with his birth certificate and his driver's licence.

Although it was only seven o'clock, he had been awake since five. First, he lay in bed and worried. Then, when he couldn't stand to be inactive any longer, he dressed and paced through the cold rooms of the house. Because it was Sunday and there was no hunting, he was afraid that Buzz

Anderson and Roger Charleston, having nothing to keep them entertained, would want to return home. Not having got their deer right away had made them discontented. Even though they hadn't complained, he could tell that it wouldn't take much for them to decide to leave. Since he was unable to think of anything else to keep them happy, he had decided to take them to the bootlegger's.

They had meant to use the entire house but they couldn't get the furnace to work so they had moved three cots into the kitchen and were heating the room with a catalytic heater.

Sonny swung open the kitchen door and let it bang closed behind him. Roger sat up and dug the knuckles of his index fingers into his eyes. He kicked himself free of his blankets and swung his feet over the edge of the cot. His legs, like the rest of him, were pale and flat looking. All he had on were jockey shorts as he sauntered over to the counter and bent down to peer outside.

"We're going to get some snow," he said.

The sky was dull grey and the distant sun was small and pale. On the horizon there was a ridge of pewter cloud.

"Good," Sonny replied. "That'll make tracking easier. You wound a deer and he'll leave a trail nobody can miss. Blood on the snow's the best thing you can have."

Roger stood on one leg, then the other, to pull on his pants. "We've got to see them before we shoot them." His voice carried a hint of irritation. He tucked in his shirt, then went back to standing on one leg to pull on his white coveralls.

"Hey, Buzz, what do you want for breakfast?" Sonny lit the Coleman stove and put on the coffee-pot.

Buzz groaned and sat up. He had on an orange toque and a matching scarf. He was constantly afraid of catching a cold or getting laryngitis and not being able to host his morning radio show for housewives. "Bacon, eggs, coffee, whisky," he said. "In that order." With a sigh, he dropped back onto the bed.

The kitchen smelled stale. The house was solid and large, with five bedrooms upstairs, four rooms downstairs and a full basement, but it had been empty for so long that the front yard was overgrown with young poplars.

After breakfast, when Sonny led the way outside, the air was sharp. The Russian thistle, touched by frost, drooped blackly. In the muted light the branches of the trees were stark and brittle looking. Huddled together on the porch, the three of them studied the dark edge of the forest that gaped toward them, then turned to study the yellows and browns of the fields that staggered toward the horizon.

"See there!" Sonny called out, punching his large red fist in the air. His two companions squinted and strained to see what had excited him, but there was nothing except the trees and weeds.

Keeping his left leg stiff, he awkwardly descended the stairs and with his massive arms moving before him in a breast stroke, swept the saplings out of his way. The other two followed him uncertainly. He snapped off the stem of a poplar and held it out for their inspection. The top had been bitten off and the tender outer bark nibbled away.

"Look at that," he said. "There were deer in here last night. Tomorrow morning we can get up early and shoot one or two from the doorway."

Buzz and Roger's interest had risen sharply and, for the moment, Sonny's worry eased. Their goodwill was crucial to him. After recuperating from a series of operations on his knee, he had become a salesman with a Ford dealership next to the stadium. He hated every minute of his fifteen years of working for someone else but by saving every cent possible, and buying and selling used cars out of his backyard, he finally managed to gather enough for a down payment on a dealership. At the same time, he moved his wife and daughter into a new house in a good neighbourhood. Then, a series of small reverses combined with too little capital squeezed him into a position where he had to have more money or lose his business.

During his two years in his new neighbourhood, he had assiduously cultivated his neighbours in the hope of turning them into customers. Now, pressed for cash, and unable to obtain further credit, he had invited Roger and Buzz on a hunting trip.

Neither of them had been deer hunting before but both had said they would like to go hunting. That, and the fact that they both had steered customers his way in return for a bottle of whisky or a pair of football tickets, made him choose them. As well, he knew from a credit check he had had run on them, that they had a fair amount of money salted away. What he intended to do was wait until they both had a deer and a few drinks and then offer to make them silent partners. He already had the papers made up.

Buzz quit studying the chewed stems and started for the car. His low, gentle voice drew women to his program in large numbers but he never allowed himself to be photographed if he could help it. He was barely five feet tall and his face—round and smooth, with slightly bulging eyes, a small, nearly bridgeless nose, red hair and freckles—made him look like a mildly retarded child.

They set off in Buzz's car, a maroon Cadillac he had bought for $200. It wasn't much to look at. The left rear door was caved in, its window held together with a black spider-web of electrician's tape. The fenders were so rusted that their edges resembled brown lace, but the motor ran well and the tires still had half a penny's width of rubber. Its major fault was that the steering was so loose that Buzz had a hard time keeping it under control.

The area they were driving through had, at one time, been the bottom of a lake. Now, a series of gravel ridges marked the successive shorelines. In the hollows, swamp grass that was the same pale brown as a red squirrel's ruff rose as high as the car windows and willow clustered in dark, impenetrable thickets. The crests were crowded with scrub oak, hazel and black poplar.

It was on the crest of a ridge that they saw a buck standing in a hazel thicket.

"Lookit that!" Roger hollered, startling Buzz so badly that he jammed on the brakes. Sonny was sitting in the back. The sudden stop nearly pitched him into the front seat.

"Look at that rack," Buzz sighed, thinking of the family room in his basement. "He's got seven points."

"I told you," Sonny said jubilantly. "I told you the way it was."

"We don't have our rifles," Roger reminded them. He had a long tubular face and the minute he was unhappy he looked like an undertaker. He pressed as close as possible to the windshield.

"I put my .22 into the trunk, remember," Sonny answered. "Give me the keys."

Buzz handed him the keys and Sonny slipped outside. Without taking his eyes off the buck, he crept to the rear of the car. Easing the trunk up slowly, he reached past the spare wheel and lifted out a rifle wound in burlap. He unwrapped it, raised it to his shoulder and squeezed the trigger. There was a sharp click.

Cursing under his breath, he tip-toed along the driver's side of the car. "Bullets," he whispered urgently. "I left them in the glove compartment."

The buck was so close that Sonny could have hit it with a rock. It stood at an angle to them, shoulder-deep in brush, its head turned sideways. The curving antlers looked polished.

"Here," Buzz said, shoving the box out of the window upside down. As Sonny snatched the box, the lid popped open and the cartridges cascaded to the ground. Sonny stood stupefied, then flung the empty box aside and scooped up a handful of cartridges and gravel. Before he could get a bullet into the chamber, the buck trotted across the road and disappeared with a bound.

Sonny fumbled a moment longer, then bitterly snapped, "Son-of-a-bitch!" He restrained an impulse to smash the car window.

As Roger and Buzz joined him, Sonny handed Roger the rifle. Then he and Buzz picked up the spilled cartridges.

"I couldn't get a bullet into the gun," Sonny explained defensively. The incident had shaken him. The buck seemed symbolic. Everything, his house, his business, his independence, seemed ready to slip away while he stood and watched helplessly.

"It was Sunday anyway," Buzz replied.

"Mounties," Roger warned. A black car had topped the adjacent ridge and was racing toward them. As Buzz and Sonny ran to the side of the road, Roger stood stupefied, then, as his long legs scissored beneath him, carrying him to safety, he flung the rifle into the bush.

Seconds later, a black Ford rocketed past, spraying them with gravel. The driver was an old woman with a green, wide-brimmed hat jammed over her ears.

With a sigh of relief, Buzz sat on a tree stump. Dramatically, he felt his heart. "You shouldn't do that, Roger. If my sponsors ever found out that I had been arrested for hunting illegally...." He left the rest unsaid.

"Where's my rifle?" Sonny asked.

Wordlessly, Roger scurried into the bush and began flailing about like a wounded duck. When he found the rifle, he waved it over his head.

To be certain the rifle was not damaged, Sonny loaded it, then fired three times. A hundred feet away, on the edge of the road, gravel flew into the air and a tin can jumped and spun on its rim before falling back. With a grunt of satisfaction, he rewrapped the rifle and stuffed it under the front seat.

Buzz brought back the can. It was pitted with rust but the edges of the bullet holes were bright and shiny. Where a hollow-nosed slug had entered, the hole was smaller than the end of a little finger. Where it exited, the hole was larger than a nickel and the edges were bent back like the sepals of a rose after the petals have fallen.

As they drove, they passed some farmhouses that, except

for the television aerials on the roofs, looked abandoned. Frequently, they saw people working among the roadside bushes. Buzz slowed down.

"What are they doing?" he asked.

"Collecting hazelnuts," Sonny answered. "They husk them and sell them to the wholesale in Winnipeg."

A man and woman were working close to the road. Each held a gunny sack. The man wore rubber boots, overalls, a brown jacket and cap. The woman wore a red *babushka*, a brown jacket and a faded dress with men's pants underneath. Two boys, dressed exactly like their father, emerged to stare at the car. Like their parents, they might have been part of the weathered landscape. From a short distance, they were nearly indistinguishable from the trees.

Buzz pulled away. "They can't get much for their work."

"They don't." Sonny was glad they were moving again. The sight of the children had been like a thrust of pain. He had been like that once. Suddenly, he could feel the weight of the scoop shovel. The stink of manure clogged his nostrils and the car seemed filled with the restless shifting of cattle.

Every morning from the time he was eight he had shovelled out the barn. In the evenings and on weekends, he hauled or pitched hay or cut wood or staggered behind the stone boat, drunk with tiredness, as he attempted the hopeless task of trying to clear the fields of their yearly crop of stone.

"What keeps people here?" Roger asked.

"Stupidity. They don't know nothing and they don't want to know nothing."

On either side, the ditches were clogged with bulrushes. Behind the ditches were hay fields, then thin lines of trees marking the edges of the fields and more trees.

"Slow down," Sonny said. "It should be along here." He was puzzled, apologetic. He had Buzz turn at the next crossroads but, after 200 yards, the road trailed away to a grassy path.

A farmhouse with the wreckage of three cars littering its front yard appeared on their right. Someone had tarpapered the outside walls and tacked on laths and chicken wire but had never put on stucco. Tattered plastic from the previous winter clung to the window-frames. The yard was adrift with chickens.

Sonny could hear the steady one-stroke beat of a small engine so he braved a black mongrel that rushed up to bare his teeth and glare malevolently from pus-stained eyes.

Behind the house, a rawboned woman in a grey shapeless dress that came to her ankles was washing clothes in a gasoline washing machine. She looked no friendlier than her dog but, when Sonny motioned to her, she moved close enough to hear what he had to say. Her face was haggard, her eyes sunken and suspicious and her hair was pinned in an untidy bun at the back of her neck. Sonny forced a smile while he tried to keep an eye on the dog, which constantly twisted out of sight.

"We've got lost. We're looking for Joe Luprypa's place," he explained.

"Down the road one mile, then turn west." Her teeth were rotted to brown stumps.

He hadn't recognized her face but he remembered her voice. He looked at her more carefully. In the lined, coarse skin there was nothing to guide him but then she said, thinking he hadn't understood. "It's that way. See. Go down to the mile road."

Annie, sprang into his mind.

He nodded and said, "Thank you. Thank you," as he backed away. Except for the voice, he was unable to see any resemblance between the girl who had sat in front of him at school and the woman with the ravaged face and raw, rough hands folded across drooping breasts.

As Sonny opened the car door, the dog lunged for his ankle but he was ready and caught it in the ribs with his foot. Joe Luprypa's driveway was deeply rutted and only wide enough for one car. It twisted down a gentle slope through a meadow of uncut hay and disappeared into a dense grove of poplars. The trees stopped at the beginning of a marsh. The car, caught by the twin ruts, was locked as securely to its path as any train. As a joke, Buzz took both hands from the wheel and clasped them behind his head. As the car bumped and rocked along the grooves in the dark earth, the wheel seemed to take on a life of its own.

In the centre of the grove there was a large patch of rutted dirt. They bounced toward a small house covered in plastic panelling that was supposed to look like natural stone. At the back of the house there was a summer kitchen painted bright purple. Permanently marching across the brown grass of the side yard to their diamond mine were plywood cutouts of the seven dwarves. An elderly blue pickup was parked to one side.

"No-one's home," Buzz said. He sounded relieved. He could listen for hours to someone else's escapades, but when he became involved in one his enthusiasm quickly cooled. "We might as well go." He studied the house apprehensively.

Sonny shoved open his door and stepped away from the car. "They're just waiting to see who we are."

The back door cracked open but they couldn't see who had opened it. Then the door was flung back and a short, fat man in charcoal-grey suit pants, a white shirt and a red flowered tie, waddled over, threw his arms around Sonny and beat him on the back. "Sonny! Long time no see. I wouldn't have recognized you except for that nose. It's still travelling in a different direction."

"We've come for a drink." Sonny waved his arm in a half-circle. "I thought there'd be no place to park."

Joe was studying Buzz and Roger closely.

"It's okay," Sonny reassured him. "They're next-door neighbours. Roger's in medicine and Buzz is in communications. Have you anything to drink?"

Joe nodded. Each time he ducked his head, he accumulated three more chins. "A little." He waved them inside.

"Go in," he urged. "What do you want? Government or homebrew? My brother, Alec, made the homebrew."

"Homebrew," Sonny replied. "I haven't had any for years."

The house smelled strongly of cabbage. Joe's wife, a dried-out woman with a disapproving look frozen to her face, cleared the table and set out three beer glasses.

The kitchen was smaller and shabbier than Sonny remembered it. It was painted bright yellow. Flowers and birds cut from magazines had been glued to the cupboards and shellacked. The windows were crammed with geraniums in red clay pots. Over the doorway to the living-room there was a plaster crucifix. The blood on it had been brightened with purple paint. From his place at the kitchen table, all Sonny could see of the living-room was a high-backed brown chesterfield layered with scalloped pink and orange doilies. Above the chesterfield in an ornate gilt frame was a paint-by-number picture of a collie.

Joe scraped his feet and locked the door behind him. "We've just come from church," he explained. He was carrying a 26-ounce bottle that was smeared with mud and grass. He held the bottle to the light and grimaced with distaste.

"We sterilize our bottles. But on the outside it's like this because of the mounties' dogs. I have to tie the bottles with a string and throw them into the marsh." He made a pulling motion with his hands. "Then I go fishing."

He rinsed the bottle under the tap. "Five dollars for this. 65 cents for tomato juice." After he pocketed Sonny's $6, Joe handed over the bottle and punched holes in a can. The tomato juice and homebrew swirled together like oil and water.

The homebrew was as raw as the cheapest bourbon. Joe brought a glass to the table and half filled it with tomato juice but his wife said, "No. His liver's bad. He's just home from the hospital," when Sonny went to add liquor.

Joe laughed to cover his embarrassment. "It must be great

to be in the city. I heard you on radio once, in a football game. Since then I heard you're doing good at cars. It's a good business. Everybody needs cars."

"It's a great business," Sonny enthusiastically agreed. He watched Roger and Buzz. "You can make a lot of money. Right now I'm ready to expand. Profits are going to be even bigger. For $10,000 I'd make someone a one-quarter partner."

Joe shook his head. "That's big money."

"It's a good investment," Sonny added. "Anybody buys in and from then on they collect while I work. No headaches, no problems, just profits."

Joe raised his glass at Roger. "Doctors always make lots of money. Somebody's always sick. That's the deal for your retirement fund."

Roger laughed off the suggestion. "Not me," he protested. "I like to put it in a nice safe bank."

"Me, too," Buzz agreed. "No risk." He gently felt his throat. "You never know when a delicate instrument might lose its tone."

Quickly, Sonny asked, "How's business for you, Joe?"

"Not good. The mounties are a problem."

"The mounties were always a problem."

Joe was downcast. He made rings on the table with the bottom of his glass. "Not like now. On weekends, in good weather, they park at the end of my driveway and sit all day. Nobody dares come. Last time, the judge said no more fines. From now on, jail. I'm too old for that."

As Joe complained, Sonny could see how much he had changed. It was not just the new lines on his face or his thinning hair. He looked worn. At one time he had been prosperous. On weekends, fifty, a hundred people came and he dispensed homebrew from a water pitcher. Then, Joe's was a place to get drunk, pick a fight or pick up a woman.

They drank steadily. At noon, Joe's wife made them roast-pork sandwiches with lots of salt and thick slices of Spanish onion. Sonny bought another bottle. By two o'clock, Roger and Buzz were very drunk. Their conversation had become so loud they were nearly shouting.

Sonny kept his glass full of tomato juice. He wanted to stay sober so that he could lead the conversation back to his dealership when the time was right. He tried to follow the conversation but couldn't because Annie kept forcing her way into his thoughts. Once he had had a crush on her. She had been pretty, with large dark eyes and a soft mouth. Now, his wife, with her trips to the health spa and the clothing stores and beauty parlour, looked like an adolescent compared to Annie. Poverty had done that. It could still do it to his wife and daughter. If he lost his dealership, the ballet, music and figure-skating lessons would be the first to go. Then the house. He was 41 and no-one would want him when they could get college kids fresh out of school.

The more he brooded about it, the worse his situation seemed. The others were so involved in their story-telling that they ignored him. Then Roger started to tell Joe about the deer. As Roger demonstrated how he got rid of the rifle, his glass slipped and crashed into the cupboard. Joe brought him a new one.

"Shooting a deer on Sunday." Joe frowned. "That's bad."

Buzz laughed and slopped his drink down the front of his coveralls. "Never mind. Sonny couldn't have hit it anyway." He stumbled from his chair and began scrambling around in a circle as he imitated Sonny's attempts to pick up the cartridges. Roger and Joe were shouting with laughter. As he turned faster and faster, like a dog chasing its tail, he shouted, "A deer. Bullets. Help. A deer."

Sonny was offended. He could see the story being told back home. Angrily, he said, "You think I can't hunt? Come on, I'll show you." He grabbed the bottle by the neck and marched outside. "I'll get a deer the way we used to."

Buzz and Roger staggered after him. A heavy, wet snow was starting to fall. Buzz drove the car to the main road. Sonny crouched in the back with the rifle sticking out the window.

"I'll show you some shooting," he said.

They swerved wildly on the slick clay. The first thing Sonny shot was a stop sign. They halted to inspect it.

"See that," he said, jabbing at the hole with his finger. "Roger couldn't do that."

"Sure, I could. Give me that rifle." Roger grabbed the barrel.

"You're in no condition." Sonny held onto the butt.

"I said give it to me." Roger's voice was belligerent. He jerked the rifle out of Sonny's hands.

The snow was beginning to fall so heavily that the countryside was blurred. They started up again and Buzz had even more difficulty controlling the car. Roger leaned so far out the car window that he looked like he was going to fall out.

"Turn left," Sonny ordered. "That's the best way. There's always deer there."

The road was so slick that they were reduced to a crawl. The snow covered the back window and clogged the windshield wipers.

"Turn here," Sonny directed. "We'll try along here."

They followed the road for over a mile, then Buzz said excitedly, "A deer."

Roger emptied the rifle as Buzz skidded to a stop.

"Did you see it?" Buzz asked. Both he and Roger started down the road. Both had difficulty keeping their balance and they walked with exaggerated care, their legs stiffly spread. With a yelp, Buzz slipped backwards and sat down in the mud. Sonny stayed in the car.

"Sonny!" Roger screamed in a high, frightened voice. "Sonny!"

When Buzz and Sonny reached Roger, he was kneeling beside a middle-aged woman in a faded brown coat with a fur collar. A man's felt cap was tied under her chin and her face was lined and shrunken. It looked like a small, dark leaf. She was an average-sized woman but lying on the ground, her legs drawn up so that only the toes of her black rubbers showed, she seemed a grotesque dwarf. Tightly gripped in her left hand was a gunny sack.

Sonny shook Roger's shoulder. "Do something. You're a doctor."

"No, I'm not." Roger replied. "I'm an optometrist."

The woman was lying on her side and a red stain was spreading over the snow at her back. The stain was as scarlet as lipstick.

"You shot her," Buzz accused him.

"You said it was a deer." Roger's voice trembled.

The woman's slack mouth tightened, then, as her lips drew back over her teeth, she gave a low, harsh cry.

"Maybe she isn't hurt bad," Roger said.

Behind them, Buzz gagged and threw up. Roger began to cry. "Lady," he said, his face stricken. "I didn't mean it."

"You shot her," Buzz repeated.

Sonny turned on him. "Shut up," he ordered. "You said she was a deer."

Snow was gathering along the woman's nose and in the folds of her coat. Except for her harsh breathing and the muted throbbing of the car's exhaust, there was no sound. They stayed absolutely still, watching the blood spread outward, becoming pink at its edge.

Just then, the woman's eyes, which had been nearly shut, opened wide and fixed fiercely upon them. Her body tensed and, for a moment, it seemed as if she would rise and strike them. Instead, her body was shaken with a violent convulsion and she rolled onto her back. After that, she was still.

"It was an accident," Roger mumbled.

"Manslaughter," Sonny replied harshly. "You were both drunk."

"We've got to get her out of here." As Buzz spoke, he began to back away. Roger hesitated, then he rose. Together, they rushed for the car. Buzz tried to open the front door on the passenger's side but his hands were trembling so violently he couldn't control them. Sonny yanked open the rear door and shoved Buzz, then Roger, inside.

The snow was falling heavily. The nearby woods were dark and endless. The air was filled with an impenetrable whiteness that isolated them in a landscape without familiar landmarks. There were no signs, not even the sun, by which to take their bearing.

"Joe," Buzz said. "He'll know."

"Joe," Sonny replied, "won't know anything. He doesn't want to go to jail." He put the car into gear.

In the back seat, Roger and Buzz stared through the windows but there was nothing except the endless whiteness. The world was blurred and indistinct and as dangerous as an uncharted coast in dense fog. Even the road was gradually disappearing.

"Where are we going?" Roger cried, his hands gripping the back seat. Buzz, his arms wrapped tightly around himself, sat hunched and mute.

Expertly, Sonny steered the car to the crest of the ridge. Roger repeated his plaintive question but Sonny, having already started them down the side of the ridge into the next hollow, was too busy to reply.

GRANITE POINT

The salt and pepper shakers were not quite aligned so Mathew grasped the salt shaker between his thumb and index finger, pushed it forward, then edged it back a fraction of an inch. "Pass the cream, please," he said.

Ellen reached the pitcher across to him. It was not real cream that he trickled over his oatmeal, but sweetened, condensed milk thinned with water. It was the twenty-eighth of May and they hadn't had fresh milk or cream since they had arrived at Granite Point the previous August.

They had dropped all pretence and Ellen never spoke unless Mathew asked her a direct question. Except for the small, sharp sounds of their spoons touching their bowls, they ate their meal in silence. Ellen would have preferred to eat when Mathew was gone but he insisted that they take their meals together so she ate mechanically, either looking at her food or studying the space just to the left or right of his head but never meeting his eyes. His eyes were small and grey and were the kind that never looked at things but peered into them as if to ferret out their smallest secrets.

Mathew was tall and angularly handsome, with black hair, a thin black moustache and an ability to look impeccable even in overalls and a red checkered shirt. Anyone seeing him for the first time with his straight posture and finely boned, patrician face would have assumed he was a young diplomat or, at least, an officer in the RAF rather than a Hudson Bay agent. Today, because it was Sunday, the store wasn't open and he was going to start building a new ice-house. The old one had been allowed to deteriorate until it would no longer keep ice over the summer. Rather than pay the Indians to help him cut and limb trees for beams, he was going to do it himself.

Ellen watched him stride to the nearby tractor and fill the gas tank from one of the red 45-gallon drums that stood in neat rows, the empty ones to the left, the full ones to the right. Only four full ones remained. Beside them, methodically arranged in ranks, were the black drums of fuel oil.

The tractor started with a series of jarring explosions that quickly ran together into a grating rhythm. Mathew jolted away and was suddenly enveloped by the dark wall of forest. The company had allotted him $3000 for a new ice-house but by building most of it himself after work and on weekends, he intended to keep the cost below half his budget. It was the type of zealousness he hoped would bring a promotion to a larger centre like Snow Lake or Flin Flon where there were roads and streetlights and fresh food all year around.

Ellen slowly cleared the table. From the window over the sink, she could see the charred outline of Kloski's house. There were the ragged edges of walls, the floor of charcoal and ashes, the buckled and rusting oil heater, the stove with one leg broken so that it leaned steeply to one corner, the brown, twisted frames of the couch and bed. She had hoped someone would clear the rubble and carry it to the dump behind the trees but no-one had and she knew that no-one would. Gradually, the burning nettle and purple fireweed would engulf it, and, later, perhaps, a thick tangle of raspberry canes would spring up.

For weeks after the fire she had washed the dishes in an enamel pan on the other side of the room so as to avoid looking at the black rectangle in the snow. There had only been a slight wind the night Kloski had splashed fuel into the stove to get the green wood started but the fire had spread so rapidly they had been unable to do anything but let it burn itself out.

There had been water, a whole lake full of it, but it was locked under four feet of ice. Even if they had chopped a hole, the water would have had to be dipped out with buckets. Conditioned to accept the inevitable, nearly the entire village stood in a semi-circle on the side of the house away from the wind. They might, except for their stillness, have been revellers around the bonfire at a winter carnival.

Not that it really mattered, the mountie who flew in to investigate had said, for Kloski was probably dead within a minute or two after the explosion. The mountie had been brisk, even impatient. He wrote his report from interviews with Mathew and Chief Albert, wrapped up the remains and rushed away before the weather closed in. Later, children playing in the debris had found melted Coke bottles. Ellen had seen them marvel as they traced the awkward shapes of slag with their fingers.

Now, the snow was gone in the open space, lingering only in the deep shade. In England it would be green but, here, everything was still yellow and grey and brown. The morning before, someone had left her a handful of willow with silver catkins just breaking their glossy casing, but, afraid of the questions Mathew would ask, she had thrown them all away except for one that she had carefully hidden beneath her side of the mattress. Ellen washed the bright blue bowls and began to scrub the sticky layer of oatmeal from the pot.

In a community as small as Granite Point, and with Kloski living next door, she had seen him several times a day but, already, without a picture of him to act as a reminder, his image was softening and fading.

When they first arrived, she was disappointed with the Indians. She had hoped they would be bright and colourful. Instead, the men and women, in their rumpled jackets and pants and ankle-length dresses, were as formless and drab as last year's leaves swept into a corner by a cold, spring rain. Behind them, the piece of granite that gave the settlement its name, thrust sharply into the lake like the prow of some massive battleship.

Behind the bare, exposed point, where they were protected by a wall of tamarack from the wind that swept down from the Arctic, was a scattering of houses. There was no break in the tree-line. It ringed the town, solid and heavy as a wall of carved slate. The sky was white and empty.

Mathew was still in the Otter, reaching out luggage. He skidded a suitcase along, accidentally striking the back of her leg. Startled, she had made a sudden movement forward, caught her toe on the rough boards and would have fallen if Kloski hadn't caught her.

"Careful," he said, his hand on her arm. "No fair getting killed before you are here a week."

He was not handsome. His face was too full and his complexion too pink. He was about 25 but his long, blond hair, his pink skin and his full, drooping moustache speckled with red hair, instead of making him look older, merely made him look like a little boy masquerading as a grownup. He was big and broad and just enough overweight that another ten pounds would have made him fat.

As Mathew stepped onto the dock, Kloski released her. They introduced themselves, then Kloski picked up a suitcase in each hand.

"Follow me. I'll show you to your place. Never mind that, Mrs. McDougal," he said when she went to lift a box. "I'll have all your belongings brought up. Everything that arrived on the boat is at your house."

He preceded them down the dock with his odd toe-out walk that made her think a little of a pregnant woman. The wall of Indians parted before him as if by magic. Without slowing down, he threw out directions in Cree.

"I asked them to bring your belongings," he explained. "See, over there? We're way over to the north side. There's my house, then your house, then your store."

All around them, like blocks dropped at random, were small, one-storey houses. Some were clapboard shacks, others were layered with tarpaper and a few were made from logs and chinked with mud. Kloski's house and their two buildings were neat, white frame structures that looked like they should have been sitting in a suburb.

"You're certain that our belongings will be safe?" Mathew asked, looking over his shoulder.

Kloski studied him a moment, then in a measured voice, said, "I've been here over two years and I've never locked my door."

"Well, I'll lock mine," Mathew replied.

They were speaking in undertones for the crowd was breaking up, some going onto the dock to ask news of the pilot, others starting to follow them back to the village. There were more huskies than people and they swirled through the crowd, evil tempered and aggressive, snarling and snapping as the larger dogs drove the smaller ones out of their way. Suddenly, with a cry of rage, a short, stocky brown dog turned on a gaunt grey with a scarred face.

Like a flock of frightened sparrows, the crowd scattered, leaving a cleared space into which the other dogs rushed to form a solid, seething mass that ebbed and flowed with the combatants. The two dogs lunged and rolled over so furiously that it was difficult to see what was happening.

"Oh, stop them!" Ellen exclaimed and impulsively started forward.

Kloski dropped a suitcase and roughly dragged her back. "Leave them be," he ordered.

"Just who do you think you're manhandling?" Mathew demanded, his voice indignant.

Kloski ignored Mathew and pulled Ellen onto a porch so they would be out of the way and Mathew, his face rigid with outrage, followed. Kloski rescued the dropped suitcase.

"Once a fight begins, one or the other has to win. There's no place else to go and if you stop it now, they'll just finish it later. That grey's been bullying the other dog all summer. If he's going to be free of him, he's got to do it himself."

Below them, the crowd had formed a circle outside the pack and, as the dogs flowed first one way, then another, advanced and retreated with them. The crowd and the dogs who were fighting were silent but the air was filled with the excited yipping of the pack.

After a flurry of attacks, both dogs pulled away and circled each other warily, their sides heaving. Their muzzles were smeared with saliva and blood. They crouched low to the ground, their legs bent; then, at the same instant, they lunged forward. The grey caught his opponent's shoulder but his teeth slipped as the brown twisted to one side and caught the grey's leg close to the body. With a vicious jerk, the brown dog knocked his enemy down and crushed his leg.

From the grey, there was a scream of terror that rose to a keening wail. Spontaneously, the pack surged forward and tore him to pieces even as he tried to pull himself free. The brown dog leaped straight into the air, turning half around, then scrambled to safety over the backs of the pack. Within minutes it was all over. The dogs barked madly and milled about before stones and sticks dispersed them. The grey dog's mutilated head was carried off by a member of the pack and all that was left were pieces of fur.

"They're half-starved," Kloski explained emotionlessly. "All they get to eat is what they find or kill or steal. If you had got in there and been knocked off your feet, there wouldn't be any more left of you than that." Although he looked at Ellen as he spoke, his words were a reprimand for Mathew.

Ellen shuddered. She thought she was going to be sick but Kloski didn't give her time. He started off so abruptly that they were both caught unawares and had to hurry after him like children. He left them and their luggage at the front door of their bungalow.

Mathew thanked him curtly. Kloski didn't quite suppress a grin.

"Insolent beggar!" Mathew exploded when they were alone. "You would think he owned the place, the way he takes charge."

Ellen leaned against the doorframe. "It was so cruel," she said.

With a start, Ellen realized she was staring out the window. It took her a moment to remember what she was supposed to be doing, then she put away the dishes. There was less than a loaf of bread left and she had to make more. She carefully wiped and dried the table, then dusted it with flour.

As she worked, she wondered what her mother would think if she could see her making bread. Before she married Mathew she seldom made her own meals. She had worked in a tobacconist's and as she lived at home, room and board cost her very little. Mr. Dowling, her employer, considered her blond hair and trim shape an asset to the store.

They were a nice class of customers he had, mostly middle-aged, and they liked a pretty girl to take the gloom off a winter's day when they stepped into the shop. She always made a point of remembering a customer's name and the brand of tobacco he liked. Each of the two Christmases she worked at Dowling's, many of the regular customers had dropped by to present her with a box of candies or cookies or a pound note. She gave most of the candy and cookies away but she added the pound notes to her savings account.

Mathew had come into Dowling's for directions. He was from Newcastle and didn't know the city. It was near closing time and since his destination was on her way, she told him to wait a moment so he could come with her. He had visited the shop the next afternoon to thank her and, at the same time, he asked for permission to call on her at home. She had agreed and he had seen her frequently after that. He was working as a clerk for one of the unions but was waiting on an application for a job in Canada. When it came, he immediately proposed. Her parents were horrified at the idea of her going so far away but his being five years older than her and his assurance that he would send her home for a long vacation the next summer, even if he could not come, had made them agreeable.

The neighbours had been unsettled by her plans to leave. The people of the area were as solid and permanent as their square brick houses. The farthest away any of the daughters of the families who lived nearby had moved was to Ireland and that, to most, seemed much too far.

At the reception, Mr. Cummins, who lived two houses away and was a special friend of her father's because of a shared passion for roses, said, "It's very isolated up there, you know. You'll have to take along something for entertainment—besides the ones newlyweds have, you know." He winked and she blushed appropriately at his being so risqué. He had gone to Canada with the army before the Second World War so he considered himself an authority on the country.

"There's canoeing and hiking and I'm going to learn ice skating," she replied. "Where we're going is right on a lake." They had a large map taped to her parents' living-room wall with a gold star at Granite Point so everyone could see where it was. Mr. Cummins had a large red nose and gout in his big toes. It was, his wife was fond of saying, the condensation of the sherry he drank.

"You'll have to learn to use a rifle and hunt and fish and all that," he advised her.

Ellen had been horrified.

"Oh, no! I couldn't do that. When a moth gets into the house I try to catch it in a jam jar and let it go outside. I couldn't kill anything."

"It's going to be quite savage," Mr. Cummins had teased before his wife dragged him away. "You'll have to be careful you don't go native." In the first letter Ellen received from home, her mother told her that Mr. Cummins' toes pained him so much that for a week after the reception he couldn't move from his chair without his canes.

"Every Sunday," Ellen had confidently said to those who had been listening, "I'm going to set a full table of china so when we come to visit we'll remember our manners. I've got pictures of Mum and Dad and all and it's only ten months before I'll be home again. It'll be as if I've never been gone."

When they left, her father, who had never been very demonstrative, surprised her by hugging her fiercely, then going quickly into the house. Her mother cried and was still waving a sodden handkerchief to and fro like a distress signal when their taxi rounded a corner.

> "Where have you been all day,
> My boy Tammie?"
> "I've been all the day
> Courting a lady gay;
> But, oh! she's too young,
> To be taken from her mammie!"

Because of the oven heating, the kitchen was stifling, but the wind from the lake was too bitter to have the door open. Remembering one verse started another. Her hands moved mechanically, spreading flour, pulling and kneading at the pale dough, but her mind raced away.

> London bridge is falling down, falling down, falling down,
> London bridge is falling down, my fair lady.
> Build it up with sticks and stones, sticks and stones, sticks and stones,
> Build it up with sticks and stones, my fair lady.

She couldn't remember the rest of it. She desperately wished she had a book of children's verses. Not to remember made her head feel squeezed tight. It was, she remembered, about the fire of London. All the houses had burned. She wondered if they had burned with such intensity as Kloski's.

The flames made a large pillar in the darkness and the crowd rippled under the wavering light like objects seen under wind-touched water. Those who were closest were outlined starkly—their eyes and buttons gleaming—while those farther back were alternately exposed and hidden like rocks in surf. Except for the dogs, which poked here and there through people's legs, nearly everyone was as stiff and unmoving as granite.

Mathew and a few others had concentrated on saving his house and store from the clouds of sparks that whirled into the air. They worked to the point of exhaustion, some banking the endangered walls while others flung snow onto the roofs where it was spread into a deep, protective layer.

Kloski was such a fool. That was what the mountie had called him for using gasoline to get his fire going. But he would have known the remaining verses. Nothing ever got him down for long. He was an encyclopaedia of trivia. Officially, he was supposed to be developing some type of steady industry to take the place of the fishing and fur trapping.

The price of fish was rising but the catch was falling. The muskrat were multiplying but the price was falling. No-one in Winnipeg or Ottawa had any specific ideas. The best they were able to do was to offer vague suggestions about developing local resources and local initiative. The local resources, besides fish and muskrat, were tamarack trees and muskeg. If he could sell someone muskeg at ten cents a foot, Kloski had said, they would all be millionaires.

Mathew found Kloski's casualness annoying. Mathew said he had no sense of propriety. Rules, Kloski replied, were made to be broken by fools like me.

Mathew ran the store with absolute efficiency, never varying from prescribed procedure. He set hours and kept a tight hand on credit purchases. The last agent had let credit too easily, depending on the bills to be paid on government day when the welfare cheques arrived. 80 per cent of the families were on welfare. When Kloski had complained about the hardship Mathew's policies were causing, Mathew replied that Indians, like anyone else, could learn to budget. He also refused to cash cheques unless ten percent of their value went to clear any unpaid balance.

In spite of their differences, Mathew and Kloski saw a lot of each other. Mathew refused to have anything to do with the Indians socially so he was happy to have Kloski come over in the evenings to talk or listen to the radio or play three-handed cribbage. After Kloski left, the house always smelled of tanned hide for he wore a deerskin jacket some of the women had made for him. The hood was fringed with timber wolf fur and the front and back were extravagantly beaded with brilliant, intricate flower patterns in red and blue and white. He also wore mukluks that someone else had made for him. The mukluks came half way to his knees and besides being encrusted with beads they were trimmed with fox fur and decorated with orange pompoms and small, circular bells that jingled whenever he moved. On still days you could hear the bells as he strolled by.

"Oranges and lemons,"
   say the bells of St. Clement's.
"You owe me five farthings,"
   say the bells of St. Martin's.
"When will you pay me,"
   say the bells of Old Bailey.
"When I grow rich,"
   say the bells of Shoreditch.

"I don't know how you can stand working with them," Mathew said over cribbage.

Here comes a candle to light.

"You work with them all the time," Kloski replied. His moustache had grown to outrageous proportions and his hair was so long that he had begun tying it back with a leather thong. Except for the area around his eyes where he was protected from snowblindness by home-made cardboard goggles, his face was burned brown. The two circles around his eyes were pink.

"No, I don't work with them," Mathew answered. "I deal with them. You associate with them. You're in one house, then another, having coffee here, bannock there. I can't imagine what you talk about."

"I'm convincing them to make mukluks and moccasins. There's a market for handicrafts. I've got to keep track of how things are going."

They alternated visits. The first time they were playing cards and having whisky at Kloski's, he went to start his wood stove to make them coffee. The wood was green and wet and didn't catch right away so he picked up a red can with a flexible nozzle and splashed some coal-oil onto it. A black twist of smoke curled up.

"You shouldn't do that," Mathew cautioned him. "You could have an explosion."

Kloski had just laughed. He had a deep, complete laugh. "I always get my fire going that way. It's coal-oil, not gasoline." He shook the can. They could hear the oil slosh about. "Got to fill it before I go to bed tonight. I don't want the heater going out on me. I'm not like some people. I don't have anyone to keep me warm."

Mathew had taken three drinks and was more outspoken than usual. "Not during the night maybe. But I've noticed all those daytime visits while the husbands are away. You're into one house, then another. Come spring, you might have some personal handicrafts produced."

Ellen could no longer stand the heat. She pulled open the kitchen door. The wind off the lake was stronger. Patches of grey rock rose from the yellow and brown grass like the backs of playful dolphins.

The ice was no longer landfast. Where a large pressure ridge had built up during the winter, ice still remained, but between this eroding rim and the pack ice that reached to the horizon, there was 300 feet of indigo water. The floes would soon be gone. All day and night they ground upon themselves.

To the right, the line of tamarack was so dark that it

seemed to have gathered into itself all the shadows of winter. Ellen pulled her cardigan more tightly about her shoulders. The houses that had been so closely joined by the snow, now that it was gone, were isolated within the circles of their own debris—empty barrels, snowmobiles, fish boxes, the spilled remnants of woodpiles. No-one was outside, for the wind was bitter. Except for two who were scavenging along the shore for dead fish, the dogs were curled in the shelter of buildings and machinery.

"The north wind doth blow,/And we shall have snow,/And what will poor robin do then,/Poor thing?" Ellen thought as she shut the door. The cold knifed to the bone. With a shiver, she moved back toward the heat.

It was right after New Year's Eve that Mathew asked Kloski to quit coming over during the day while he was not at home. Ellen had not known about it until one afternoon when, as she was brooding and wanted cheering up, she heard the jingle of Kloski's bells and had rushed to the door to ask him in.

"Coffee?" she asked eagerly.

He never turned down the offer of coffee. Mathew said it was because he was a loafer and had even suggested that it might be because Kloski had native blood.

"Not right now," he replied.

Her disappointment was so great that she felt her face crumple.

"I'm sorry," he apologized in a quiet, almost shy voice, and went on his way, leaving a trail of toed-out footprints in the snow.

She was so hurt, she cried. At supper, hoping that Mathew might fix whatever was wrong, she told him what had happened.

"I asked him not to come," Mathew said matter-of-factly.

"But why?" she asked.

Mathew never liked having to explain things. Somewhat stiffly, he answered, "Because it doesn't look right. There's talk all over the village about how he stops to visit with the women for hours on end. That may not matter to the others but I won't have that kind of talk about my wife. We have our positions to uphold."

"But he's the only person I see besides you," she protested. "I've got to see someone. I can't just sit here as if I was in prison."

"It's my house and he won't come unless I ask him." Mathew's face had become flushed.

"Then I'll go to his house," she retorted, her lips trembling.

He hit her. His hand caught her on the mouth. She touched the corner of her lips. When she looked at her fingers, the tips were smeared with blood.

"When I go home, I won't come back." She rose from the table and went to the sink to soak a cloth in cold water. Defiantly, she added, "I'll visit whoever I want."

That had been after New Year's. They had all spent Christmas and New Year's together. At Christmas, Kloski had supplied a venison roast. She made Yorkshire pudding and plum pudding with custard sauce. Kloski gave Mathew a cribbage board made from the prong of a deer antler. For her he had a pair of beaded doeskin slippers. In return, they gave him a bottle of rum and a box of English toffee. For New Year's they had gone to his place. He had a hot rum punch ready for them. Mathew brought his new cribbage board and she brought her slippers to wear around the house.

Christmas had been fun but New Year's was melancholy. To make it good, they needed more people. They sat up until midnight, not saying much and drinking more than they should. At twelve, Ellen had kissed Mathew. Kloski had clumsily pecked at her cheek. She had thrown her arms around him and, laughing at his embarrassment, had refused to let go until he kissed her properly.

At the door, as he said goodnight to them, Kloski repeated his old joke by shivering and saying, "I'll have to be sure the fire doesn't go out. What'll I do if it gets really cold?" It was twenty below.

"He'll sit in the barn/And keep himself warm/And tuck his head under his wing,/Poor thing!" She was staring at the remains of the house again. The charred foundations rose like black mountains seen from a great distance. She turned away.

She fitted the dough into a large, yellow bowl, covered it with a clean white towel and left it to rise. She looked at the clock. It was noon hour. Mathew should be back soon. She took the rest of the bread, sliced it, then cut slices from yesterday's roast and made sandwiches. She put on water to boil for soup.

There wasn't going to be any money for going home this year. She had no idea how much money Mathew made or had saved but all she had were two one-pound notes that she had brought as keepsakes. Even if she had a thousand, they wouldn't have done her any good. No-one here knew what they were. Anything she needed, Mathew brought from the store but she never saw any cash. Not a penny. And her mother's letters and her own all had to pass through Mathew's hands for the store was also the post office. When her mother's letters arrived, they were always open.

In defiance of Mathew, she had gone to visit Kloski the next day. He was not at home but his door was always open so she went inside and waited till he appeared. Her mouth was swollen and the tea he made for her hurt but Kloski didn't comment on her swollen lip. They silently played double solitaire. Mathew had burst in without knocking and ordered her home. She was terrified but she refused to budge. When Mathew grabbed her arm and tried to drag her to her feet, Kloski, like a large, clumsy bear, caught Mathew's arms just below the shoulders and shook him until he was helpless. Then Kloski sat Mathew down in a chair beside the door and returned to the card game. When Mathew recovered enough to stand, he stumbled outside. Neither of them looked up.

Lunch, Ellen thought, Mathew should be coming home

for lunch. When she looked out she saw that something had drawn the dogs from their shelters. She was too restless to sit so she pulled on her parka. She couldn't see any sign of Mathew so she started walking toward the trees, following the ruts made by the tractor.

She was afraid of the forest. It was like a dark tunnel with no ending. Where the land was high, it was closely packed with tamarack, with their sharp, jutting branches that threatened your eyes. Where the land was low, muskeg shivered underfoot. She went slowly for the granite was slippery with moss and lichen and the muskeg sucked at her feet. Twice, she stumbled. As she walked, dogs dashed past her, crossing and recrossing the path made by the tractor. The farther she went, the more dogs there were and the more excited they were until it seemed as if all the dogs of the village were hurling themselves in a frenzy through the bush.

Just ahead, on a rise where there was a grove of birch, there was an excited, expectant yipping. Four trees had been felled and limbed. The yellow tractor stood in the middle of the small clearing. Mathew's head protruded above it.

Ellen circled around to the far side of the tractor. Mathew had been doing something with the motor and had caught his hand in the machinery. Blood had caked in long streaks down his arm. With his free hand, he held a length of branch. Some dogs were running excitedly back and forth but others were lying patiently in a semi-circle just out of reach of his club. As she watched, one of the dogs lunged forward and slashed at Mathew's leg. His club thumped awkwardly to the ground and he cried out with the pain. His pants were torn half-way to his knee.

He saw her then.

"Ellen!" he called with sudden hope. "Ellen!"

The dogs, aware of her presence, began to watch her.

"Get the axe," he cried, "and cut the belt." He was bound to the tractor by a taut, wide belt that had crushed his hand. The axe lay on the ground just out of reach of his club. Its head gleamed as brightly as polished silver. All around, the trees pressed close, making the clearing smaller.

She felt as if she was going to fall and stretched both arms out from her shoulders to keep her balance. She could see Mathew so clearly that the veins of the hand with which he gripped the tree branch stood out like ridges and the dark hair rose stiffly over his knuckles. At the same time, he seemed distant, beyond her reach, constantly shrinking. She pushed one foot toward him, craning her neck forward, then stopped, squinting suspiciously.

"Ellen," he pleaded, "help me." His voice was small with pain and fear and his lips worked convulsively even when there was no sound.

Where Mathew's pants were newly torn, she could see the line of bright blood. There was a rat, a mouse and a little froggee, she remembered. She concentrated intensely, trying to remember why she had come. *Lunch*, she thought, *he won't be able to come for lunch.* She studied the red smear where his hand disappeared beneath the rough-textured belt. The blood was brighter than she had ever imagined blood being, as bright as the gasoline barrels.

"Lift up the axe. Cut the belt." He was pleading with her as he might with a child. "It's just a little thing. Please."

She had thought that much blood would be darker, nearly black. Like the oil barrels. Like what had been left of Kloski. They had stood in front of her so she could not see but they had not been quick enough.

The dogs had slowed. Their movements were no longer so abrupt. They still circled and twisted but they moved more rhythmically, their eyes on her, watching her every movement. Their barking had become muffled. She could see the strength in their legs and shoulders. Their muzzles were wet.

Mathew reached the branch toward her with the gentleness of an offering. It did not touch her. To gain her attention, he flicked it, striking her cheek with the tip of a twig. Involuntarily, she jerked back and clasped her hand to her cheek, her eyes momentarily focusing on her husband.

"Ellen!" he exclaimed hopefully.

She swayed back and forth, in danger of losing her balance. Catching herself, she turned and hurried away without looking back.

SAVED

"For heaven's sake, Melissa, offer them something cold," Ernest Sanderson said.

He was stretched out over the kitchen counter, squinting past a corner of the curtain at the four women who had spent the morning painting the church. Except for a slight difference in height, they looked identical. They all wore brown ankle-length dresses with high collars and long sleeves and each one had her hair braided, coiled and pinned in a bun at the nape of her neck. He had checked on them every half-hour and had watched the sun, blazing whitely in a cloudless sky, press on them like some great weight until it had reduced their quick, graceful movements to awkwardness. When they had first come, they had sung hymns in high, clear voices. For the last two hours they had been silent.

Melissa studied the hand of solitaire spread before her. "Suffering is good for the soul," she said. "Mortifying the flesh and all that."

"Do you know how hot it is out there?"

The question was rhetorical. The last tenants had left a thermometer nailed to a window-frame and only a minute before he had read her the temperature. It was 92. The heat was so oppressive that all Melissa had on was a floor-length apron with a small bib. A strap that slipped over her head and two ribbons that tied at the small of her back held it in place. The edges of the apron left a two-inch vertical gap. Her short blond hair, damp with perspiration and humidity, was curled tightly along the side of her face. She was of medium height, with a good shape, soft pink skin and eyes the colour of pale amethyst.

"All they've got is a gallon of water they brought in a glass jar. By now it must be steaming." When she paid no attention, his voice grew peevish. "It wouldn't hurt to do them a favour."

For the last two hours he had been wanting Melissa to take the women something to drink and she had steadfastly refused. Because she was a naturally generous person, if the building had been anything but a church, she would have been carting drinks back and forth all morning. But ever since Ernest had first met her, she would have nothing to do with churches or ministers. She felt so strongly against religion that she went to incredible lengths to avoid any kind of contact with it. It was, she had grudgingly admitted to Ernest's persistent questioning, because her father had been a fundamentalist preacher. He had taken her from one revival to another in an erratic journey that only ended when she stole one night's offering and fled on the first available bus. Her *call* had been to save children. As soon as she was free, she had ruthlessly cast off her old role and when Ernest had met her she was working as a waitress at the student union and posing in the nude for art classes. They had lived together for a year. When he finally got a job, they went to the courthouse to be married.

As he watched her work her way through the deck of cards, his resentment grew. He had taken a job he disliked intensely and he felt that since he had made a sacrifice the least she could do was make an attempt to co-operate.

"It wouldn't hurt," he repeated. "Like it or not, the way the job market is we're going to have to stay here, two, three years."

He slapped his hands down over the cards. She leaned back and waited.

"Look, all I'm saying is let's be nice to them. It doesn't cost anything to be nice. We need this job. If I'm going to get something else, I need good recommendations."

She tipped back her head to stare at him. Her eyes were expressionless.

Exasperated, he jumped up and mixed the Kool-Aid himself. Since all he was wearing was a pair of madras shorts, before he went out he slipped a shirt over his narrow shoulders. His arms and legs were thin and covered with black hair.

The sun was a fierce white ball. The wild hay that surrounded the house was so limp that it slumped upon itself. The women had settled in the shade of an elderly truck, the bed of which had served them as a scaffold. They sat in a square, their heads bowed and their eyes shut as they said grace over a shoe-box filled with sandwiches and a gallon pickle jar half filled with water.

Ernest was surprised to see that, in spite of the way they were dressed, they were no older than Melissa. None of them wore makeup and their pink faces were as curved and smooth as water-worn stone. Perspiration stained the collars and underarms of their dresses.

As the girl opposite him looked up, Ernest quickly said, "My wife and I thought you might like something cold." They eyed him suspiciously so he quickly added, "There's nothing in it except water and sugar and raspberry flavouring." Not knowing what else to do, he held out the jug. To his relief, the girl closest to him accepted it.

Ernest turned quickly and had the satisfaction of seeing the kitchen curtain fall into place. Melissa, in spite of her professed disinterest, had been watching. When he entered, she did not look up, but sarcastically said, "Hail Samaritan."

"Lay off," he replied. "It's not funny."

She shrugged. The bib of her apron puckered away from her body so that, from the side, her small, firm breasts were completely bare. She was as sleek and sinuous as a cat. Normally, her action would have aroused him; now, it annoyed him. He felt that though she said nothing, she blamed him for the fact that he had rented a house next door to a church.

He felt she was being unfair, for nearly anyone would have been fooled by its appearance.

It was small and narrow, with a steep shingle roof, no windows, no cross. The pale yellow pine was so new that it looked like pale honey. A metal chimney, front and back steps, and a heavy twist of black power line that hung like a gigantic licorice whip from one corner, were the only things that broke the building's symmetry. He knew there were no waterworks for behind the building, spaced well apart, were two outhouses. Beside them, piles of clay glistened like fresh putty.

They had only found out it was a church when they had gone shopping at the Clover Leaf store.

"That bunch," the jowly butcher had said, "that has the church next to you, don't have anything to do with them. He was short and heavy set and constantly wiped his bloodstained hands on his white apron. "A whole colony of those Mennonites moved in two years ago. Some said they'd be good for the town." He snorted with skepticism. "You the new teacher?"

Ernest nodded.

"Up till this year, they stopped at grade eight. Smart, dumb, didn't make any difference. This year they've sent a slew of kids to grade nine. That's why we needed another teacher. Don't get too settled," he warned. "They think everything's a sin. They'll probably take their kids out lickity-split when they come home thinking something new." He weighed and wrapped their pork chops in white paper, then scribbled on the price with a grease pencil.

Ernest stopped to peek at the girls from time to time during the day but he was caught by surprise at five o'clock by a gentle knock. When he answered it, the girl who had accepted the jug was waiting on the top step. She had a narrow, foxy face and small, inquisitive eyes. Her cheeks were the flaming, hard red that presages heat stroke.

After she had gone, Ernest said to Melissa, "See, it didn't do any harm."

The next morning, a light knocking awakened them. Before Ernest could find his pants, Melissa pulled on her housecoat and stumbled down the hallway.

"Who?" he mumbled when she returned.

"The Kool-Aid Kid," she replied crossly as she climbed into bed. They had gone to bed half drunk on chianti and she had a headache. "She wants to use our outdoor tap." As if to confirm her statement, there was the harsh squeal of air in the pipes, then the drumming of water on the bottom of a metal pail.

On Sunday morning at ten o'clock, when Ernest was making coffee, the four girls drove up in an elderly blue Ford. To his horror, he saw them looking toward the house. He had shaved but he wasn't dressed.

The supper dishes and an empty whisky bottle were piled on the cupboard. "Melissa," he shouted. "Get up. We've got company." Yanking open the oven door, he recklessly shoved the dishes and bottle into the stove. Then he raced down the hallway. He found Melissa standing, dazed, in the middle of the bedroom.

"What?" she asked.

"They're coming, they're coming," he gasped as he dragged a shirt and pants out of the closet. Melissa grabbed a dress and pulled it over her bikini pyjamas, jammed her feet into a pair of shoes and was frantically brushing her hair when the first knock sounded. Ernest started down the hallway, first on one foot, then the other, as he tried to tie his laces. At the doorway he gave up and stuffed the laces into the sides of his shoes. When he opened the door, a cluster of pale, round faces was waiting.

"We have come to repay your kindness," the Kool-Aid Kid announced very formally and handed him a plucked chicken, its head, feet and viscera still intact. Ernest instinctively grasped it by the neck so that it dangled limply between them as the girl introduced herself and the others.

"I'm Elizabeth Friesen." She pointed out the others in descending order of age. They were Rachel, Leah and Ruth.

All four wore shapeless purple dresses that left only the skin of their hands and faces bare.

"Thank you. That's very kind of you." He knew he should do something but his concentration was wrenched between a need to stall for time and a need to get rid of the chicken, which revolved slowly like a hanged man. Hearing Melissa behind him, he gratefully turned to her. "Look what they brought us," he said shrilly, holding the chicken at arm's length. He did not remember ever having seen a chicken with feet before. The head hung limply over his hand. The bird spun, stopped, and began to spin back. "Why don't you show your guests into the living-room?" he suggested.

As Melissa led the girls through the archway, he laid the chicken out on the stove. They had no living-room furniture so he carted in four chairs for the girls and pressed the kitchen stool and their leather hassock into service.

The visit was painful. Each girl sat rigidly in her chair, her hands folded on a large black Bible. Ernest wondered, because of the position of the book, whether it was a charm to protect their virtue.

Melissa, who normally faced crises with casual ease, was so rattled by the visit that she rushed at one subject after another. She was like someone playing blind man's buff. He listened in amazement until he realized that she was trying desperately to keep their guests from discussing religion. Listening to her was painful but Ernest was unable to come to her rescue because he couldn't remember anything about farming except for a picture from grade school showing six combines in a row, that the short-grass plains started in Saskatchewan, and that in Russia they were called the steppes.

"How are things on the farm?" he asked.

"Good," Elizabeth replied and the others nodded and echoed, "Good." They did not elaborate.

While they were distracted, Melissa fled to the kitchen to make lemonade.

"You worked hard the other day."

"It was our duty," Elizabeth replied. "We were sick afterward." Ernest thought he detected a hint of smugness in her voice.

"Couldn't you have put it off for another day?"

"Christ did not shirk the cross. He did not put off Man's salvation for another day."

"It was our duty," the others echoed.

Unable to think of an intelligent answer, he changed the subject. "Some of your people are going to school this fall."

All four studied him in stony silence, then Elizabeth answered, "Yes."

Fear seized him. He wondered if he had inadvertently offended them. "Do you not approve?"

"We shall see," Elizabeth replied ambiguously.

Melissa appeared with a tray of drinks. Ernest fidgeted with his glass until he was sure they weren't going to say grace. They drank their lemonade quickly and, all together, as if they had rehearsed it, rose to leave. Hastily Ernest clambered to his feet.

"Tonight, we'd like to call and take you to our church. It will be the first time we have used our new building."

He felt, rather than heard, Melissa's indrawn breath. Deliberately, he shifted so he couldn't see her. The four smooth faces seemed to press close, demanding an answer. "Yes," he said, "of course, we'd be glad to come." He showed them to the door.

When he came back, Melissa was busy picking up glasses. Defensively, he said, "I had to accept. You heard the way they feel about their people going to school." She ignored him. "If it wasn't for them, we wouldn't be married."

"I wasn't the one who wanted to get married."

"Weren't you?" Stung by the implication that marrying him did not matter to her, he snapped cruelly, "What would you have done when I left? Moved in with someone else? Like Marj?" Marj was 30, a one-time cheerleader who had been handed from graduate student to graduate student for the past twelve years. "I can't help your stupid phobias. I didn't make your old man nuts. Oh, yes, I love you," he mimicked her. "Sure you do. Just so it doesn't cost you anything."

His accusation wasn't fair and, when he saw her face tighten with pain, he was sorry. There was no pleasure in hurting her. Lamely, he added, "You have to compromise sometimes."

Instead of starting to wash the glasses, she picked one up and put it down absentmindedly. "I'd better leave," she said.

At an earlier time, her mentioning leaving would have frightened him, but now it did not. She had no way of leaving. She didn't drive and the only money they had was in travellers' cheques in his name. She was frightened of hitchhiking. He knew how insecure she was because of the way she had lately started at unfamiliar sounds and stayed close to the house. If her fears about religion had been more rational, if her danger more real, he would have been able to muster some sympathy. Secretly, he harboured the belief that what she needed was to face up to her problem and overcome it and he was not unhappy that a crisis was approaching.

"I don't want you to leave," he said honestly. "I want you to stay. I married you because I wanted us to be together."

The stormy, emotional scene he had expected did not materialize. Instead, she filled the sink and began to wash the glasses. In a gesture of reconciliation, he picked up a tea towel and began to dry.

Then, to his dismay, she said in an abstracted manner he had never heard her use before, "I'll be leaving in a little while."

When he went to the bedroom, he stood in the hallway listening for the click of suitcases being opened. Hearing nothing, he peeked in. She was sitting on the edge of the bed with her back to the door.

She didn't come out to make supper but Ernest didn't mind. He was too nervous to eat. They could, he thought, after it was over, have a late meal of spaghetti and wine. He had a little marijuana hoarded. They could have a smoke and relax. At 7.30, he began to get dressed. "Hey, it's time to go," he said.

Melissa hadn't moved but as soon as he spoke she pulled on a long dark skirt, a blue blouse and a black sweater. When she came out of the bathroom, her face was devoid of makeup and the curl had been ruthlessly tugged from her hair. He didn't like the way she looked and wished that she had used a little something, not enough to be noticeable, but enough to emphasize her good points.

When they entered the church in the company of the four girls, it was nearly full. The men, dressed in black, sat on the left, and the women, in dull browns and blues, sat on the right. Elizabeth led them proudly to a seat near the front. Ernest would have preferred to sit at the back where he wouldn't have felt so conspicuous.

The inside of the church was as plain as the outside. Ernest had survived Catholic masses by studying statues of angels in flight, saints pierced thickly with arrows, windows ablaze with colour; here, there was only a small, plain box filled with rows of backless benches. He would, if he could, have stared out a window at a bird or a tree but there were only blank white walls.

When the shuffling of entering feet stopped, one of the men began singing. There was no organ but there was no need of it as the congregation joined in with fervour. After three hymns, a man with a long, square jaw and large ears that cupped forward, stood and faced the congregation. His face was burnt reddish-brown.

"There are no procrastinators in Heaven," he began, his voice challenging the congregation. Ernest let his eyes wander but there was nothing to see. All distractions had been eliminated. He would have liked to study the people around him but in the small room he was a prisoner of simplicity. Every move he made could be seen.

How, he wondered, were the gangling sons and pale daughters of Hellfire going to take to Darwin? With a flash of insight, he realized his hope for the next year had no foundation. Truth would drive them from the classroom, if not the truth he dispensed in history, then the truth of biology or literature. They would come, suspicious, uncertain, and long before the year was out, would leave, their worst fears confirmed.

Aware that forces beyond his control were going to keep him from a permanent job, he tapped Melissa's foot. When she did not respond, he glanced at her. Her body was rigid, her eyes fastened to the speaker who paced rapidly back and forth, pounding out the word of God on the palm of his left hand. *The Bible, Ernest thought, written in English by the hand of God. The simpletons probably did not know it had been translated.* Inwardly, he groaned.

Abruptly, the speaker stopped. Surprised, Ernest felt the same wave of guilt he had felt when he was a child and his grade-three teacher had stopped a lesson because he was talking.

In the far corner, a second man stood. He, like the first, was tall and windburnt. He had a large nose and a small, receding chin and his wrists hung inches below his sleeves. He said nothing, but stood before the congregation, his hands at his sides. With a barely perceptible movement, he met the eyes of the man nearest him. With careful deliberateness, he went from one man to the next. Some looked down, others turned away, but a few met his gaze. Some, he spent no more than a second or two on; others, he stayed with for a minute or more. The silence was replaced with a nervous rustling.

When he had finished with the men, he crossed to the women. One of those in front of Ernest dropped her chin to her breast and would not look up. A young girl began to cry as he approached. Beside him, Ernest felt Melissa stiffen.

This is ridiculous, he thought. He was sorry he had come. *Never again,* he promised himself.

When his turn came, he had no impression of a face, but only of blank grey eyes in which he saw his own reflection.

After a few seconds, a small panic began to unfold deep inside him. Instead of looking away, he reverted to a trick from his childhood that he'd used to defeat nightmares. He began to think about Donald Duck doing something funny. With that, the man moved on.

When the search was over, the original speaker rose and asked, "How many of you feel Christ inside you? How many of you have been touched by His presence tonight?" He spread his arms wide, his palms up. Standing to one side, keeping them all in sight, was their silent inquisitor.

Ernest half-expected the congregation to rise as a body, the way they did in the Lutheran church of his childhood. Instead, they sat, rigid chips of dark wood. Finally, with a rustle of cloth, a middle-aged woman rose. The silence tightened around them. Ernest could hear his own heart. *I will*, he solemnly promised himself, *apologize and make amends*.

A man in the front row stood. Slowly, hesitantly, others followed suit.

Elizabeth rose but her sisters did not. Ernest could feel Melissa tremble violently. She shifted twice and, each time, Ernest thought she was going to stand. The silence tightened once more. No-one moved. At last, the man at the front released the upright bodies by turning his palms toward the floor.

The benediction was mercifully brief. When Ernest turned to Melissa, he saw that her face was pale, her lower lip beaded with sweat. Shocked, he caught her elbow and gave it a brief, reassuring squeeze.

As they slowly edged toward the door, the crowd separated him from his wife. At the threshold, Melissa whispered briefly to the preacher. Ernest was going to speak to the man who had looked into his eyes but Elizabeth touched his arm. "He cannot talk or hear," she whispered.

He was relieved that it was over and he wanted to be left alone with Melissa but, to his annoyance, the four girls walked them to the back door. On the horizon, a string of clouds was deep purple and the rim of the sun was a scarlet curve. He said goodnight so sharply that it bordered on rudeness.

Inside the door, he sighed with relief. Keeping his promise, he said, "I'm sorry. We shouldn't have gone."

Melissa stood before him without moving, her arms folded.

"Look, I'll get changed and I'll make us some supper. I've given you a bad time and I know it. Okay, I admit it." He went to her and pulled her into his arms. Passively, she accepted his kiss. "As soon as I change, I'll make some pizza and we'll have some wine and a smoke."

As he was talking, he hurried to the bedroom, raising his voice as he went. His jacket and shirt were off when he heard the kitchen door shut. "Melissa?" he called. "Is someone there?"

There was no reply. He ran to the kitchen. It was empty. He flung open the door. In the gathering gloom, he saw Melissa hurrying into the church. He ran after her and pounded up the stairs but the door was slammed in his face by the deaf mute. Before it closed, he saw his wife, kneeling at the preacher's feet, her face pressed into her hands.

He kicked the door with all his strength but it was solidly built. Although it shivered under his assault, it did not break. In the hope that they had forgotten there was a rear entrance, he ran to the back door but it, too, was locked.

"Melissa!" he yelled over and over as he ran, first to one side, then the other, but his wife was enclosed by locks and bars he could neither break nor open and hidden by walls through which he could not see.

IN MANITOBA

As each man entered the cookshack, he dragged a chair from the table, sat down and began to fill his plate from the platters of food that were set out. Harold Wolk, a short, sinewy man of 50, with small, close-set eyes and a narrow chin, took three fried eggs, then ignoring his boss's glare of disapproval as he reached for a fourth, said, "Valdi, you've got a visitor."

Valdi Gudmundson, the camp owner, was watching his wife, Runa, pack the lines of black lunch buckets with sandwiches. He went to the side window and looked out, but there was nothing to see that was not ordinarily there—the beetle-shaped bombardier under its tattered covering of black plastic, a mound of hay bales, the woodpile, the tractor. Except for the area beside the woodpile, which was covered with a deep layer of sawdust, the ground had been churned to mud that had been frozen into deep ruts. Where the sun touched them, the trees were yellow and red, but below that ragged band of colour, the shadows were thick and solid.

"Where? I don't see anyone," he replied with annoyance. He was large and husky but his skin was pale with a grey cast to it around his eyes and mouth.

"Beside the door," Harold said, waving his fork. "There's an Indian."

Valdi eyed Harold suspiciously, as if expecting a joke at his expense. "What does he want?"

Harold shrugged. "We didn't stop to talk."

Valdi studied the other four men who were hunched over

their plates. They were too busy eating to speak, but two of them confirmed Harold's statement by nodding. Valdi went back to the counter. Runa set each plaid thermos into its lunch basket, then snapped the lids shut. While they were still chewing the last of their breakfast, the men hurried out.

Runa cleared the table, then poured herself a cup of coffee. She was twenty-five, fifteen years younger than her husband. She was pretty, with a smooth well-tanned skin, moss-green eyes and blond hair that she wore in a single braid down her back. As she sat at the table, she rolled four cigarettes, put three into her shirt pocket and lit one.

"I wonder what he wants," Valdi said. A fly, roused by the heat from the stove, began to bang stupidly against the window-pane. Valdi stood, killed it with the flick of a dish towel, then leaned against the window. The angle was too great for him to see if anyone was still there.

Valdi took the dishpan and threw the dirty water outside. As he did so, he looked over the Indian who was squatting beside the door. He was young, no older than 21 or 22 and had skin the colour of light caramel. He had strong features —a high forehead, smooth dark hair, heavy eyebrows and a mouth that was a little too large to allow him to be handsome.

"What do you want?" Valdi demanded.

"Work." The Indian's voice was so quiet that it was barely audible. Having glanced at Valdi, he looked away, as if to create a great distance between them as they talked.

"Why did you come here?"

"I heard you had a man injured."

It was true. One of Valdi's men had crushed his hand two days before.

Valdi studied the breadth of his shoulders, his leanness, his olive bedroll, his battered suitcase held together with twine. His denim jacket, jeans and red flannel shirt were old but clean and his work boots were shiny new.

"You fished before?"

"On Great Slave."

"Not here?"

He shook his head.

"Who'd you fish for?"

"Jack Simondson. Fusi Bergman."

Valdi caught his lower lip between his thumb and index finger and drew it out. He desperately needed another man. In another day, the fish in the injured man's nets would begin to rot.

"What's your name?"

"Elliot Household."

"I don't usually hire Indians."

Elliot's face was impassive. Runa appeared in the doorway behind her husband. The sun had risen above the trees but the light it gave off was thin and weak.

"You think you can catch fish?"

"Yes."

Valdi pulled at his lip. "No wages," he said finally. "70 percent for us, 30 for you. You get your money when the nets are on shore the last day of the season. Board and room."

"All right."

The proposal was so unfair that to cover up his surprise at the ready agreement, Valdi walked brusquely to the storage shed next to the cookshack. Elliot rose and followed him. There were no windows so Valdi left the door open to give them light. Winter fishing equipment was strewn about.

"You can clean yourself a place. There's cots and mattresses in back." At the door, he turned and said, "You keep your hands off the supplies."

When he returned to the kitchen, Valdi sat looking out the window, his eyes locked on a dead birch.

Runa was knitting and her slender fingers flashed in a steady rhythm. The click of the needles was so regular that there seemed to be no pause. Even when her attention was elsewhere, her hands moved automatically. She was knitting heavy woolen mittens for the winter fishermen. Valdi resented her having to make the mittens but they needed the money too badly for him to say anything.

She didn't ask what was bothering him. Before a heart attack had put him in the hospital for three months the year before, he had been even tempered, but since then he had brooded constantly, sometimes refusing to speak for days at a time. Without warning, he would erupt in fits of violent temper.

At last, he said, "That Indian's a liar. His hands haven't got a callous on them." He twisted agitatedly in the chair. "Get a lunch ready for him."

Twenty minutes later, Valdi was on the lake with Elliot in the stern. Valdi sat backward in the bow, watching every move Elliot made.

Elliot handled the 22-foot skiff skilfully and when they reached the first buoy with its red float and white, numbered flag he eased alongside, grasped the pole and held onto it as he and Valdi changed places. He gathered the lines and began to pull the boat along, hand over hand, in the direction of the second buoy, which marked the far end of the gang of nets.

The lake was silent and still, a great flat surface as faded as a blanket laundered until its colour is nearly lost. The boat, jerked forward hand over hand, repeatedly shattered its own white image. Less than half a mile away, a series of small crescents and points were smoothly fastened to the water. Farther back, a line of frost-burned trees pressed darkly together.

When Elliot reached the far buoy, he had half a dozen fish. Three of these were small, silver sunfish of no value. Elliot rinsed his hands in the cold water and after briskly rubbing them on his pants, asked, "Where now?"

When they reached an area half a mile to the north, Valdi drew a grappling iron and coil of rope from a fish box beneath the seat. He dropped the grappling iron overboard. Following Valdi's directions, Elliot ran the boat back and forth parallel to the shore. On their third pass, the rope went taut and Elliot turned off the motor.

Once again, he and Valdi changed places. As Elliot hauled in the rope a dark line of corks broke the nearby surface. Catching the net, he freed the grapple, then lifted the mesh until the lead line appeared. He spread one square of mesh with his thumb and index finger.

"Two and a quarter inches," he said.

"What if it is?" Valdi demanded, shielding his eyes with his cupped hand. His eyes looked sore and red. "You want to fish on shares for that?" He waved his pale hand contemptuously at the fish that flopped dispiritedly on the bottom of the boat.

It was a poor catch. Reluctantly, Elliot began lifting. In the first two fathoms there were five pickerel.

"Some difference?" Valdi asked, hooking two fingers into a pickerel's gills and holding it up so that its green, irridescent back sparkled in the sun. "40¢ a pound for those," he said slyly. "A man could make a little money. We've got sixteen gangs of ten nets of small mesh. You get two gangs. Don't let anything happen to them. I had to borrow on my camp to buy them."

After Valdi showed Elliot where the other gang of small mesh was and pointed out the legal nets, Elliot took him back to shore. Then he returned and finished lifting.

Supper was eaten in silence. The men never were talkative, but Elliot's presence made the silence constrained and awkward. While the men ate, Runa carried in firewood for the cookstove and filled the water barrel by carrying water from the lake. Normally, she would have had a cookee to do the chores, but this year, to save money, she did them herself.

Throughout the week, while the weather deteriorated, the catch increased. What started as a light breeze increased steadily until large, grey waves crashed along the shore and the air was filled with cold, hard spray.

On Sunday, at the supper table, Harold broke the silence long enough to say, "There's still sign of that damn sunfish. Every day I've been getting five pounds more than the last. With that wind from the south, we could get a run and then we'd be in a hell of a mess."

Valdi had noticed the sunfish but because he was afraid of missing even one day's catch, he didn't want the nets pulled. "We leave the nets in. It's too late in the season for sunfish."

"We keep getting signs," Harold persisted, shaking his scrawny finger at Valdi.

Valdi ignored him.

The next morning, the clouds were low and black and they travelled very fast in ragged sections. Blowing furiously, the wind swept everything before it. While the others played cards, Elliot, dressed in bulky pants and jacket, his face obscured by a black, wide-brimmed hat tied beneath his chin, clambered down to the dock.

Counting the seconds between the waves, he waited, then, as the seventh wave broke, he raced down the dock through ankle-deep water and jumped into his boat. Ignoring the sheets of spray that swept over him, he started the engine and drove the boat straight into the waves. Late in the day when he returned, his boat was half full of water and his nets were crammed in tight piles between the seats.

As Elliot carried his nets to the sheltered side of the storage shed, Valdi said to Runa, "Bloody stupid Indian. What does he think he's doing? He could have swamped and lost everything."

The next day the lake was whipped to a frenzy. Elliot, after making a crude shelter from fish boxes, began to spread and clean his nets. After lunch, Runa came outside to split wood. The axe head was too heavy and the handle too long so that she swung awkwardly, twice striking glancing blows that nearly drove the blade into her leg.

Runa was startled when Elliot reached from behind her to grasp the handle. She released the axe and turned toward him. Her face was pink from the wind and her breathing was heavy and fast from her exertion. Each time she breathed, her nostrils flared and her breasts, under her nylon windbreaker, rose and fell noticeably.

"I'll do that," he said. He set a block on end and split it with one blow. With quick, sure strokes, he cut each half into three parts. He picked up the pieces and piled them into her arms.

Unused to such favours, she didn't know what to say. They stood, looking at each other for another moment, but then Runa saw Valdi watching them and scurried away. Elliot turned his back on Valdi and, during the next two hours, split enough stove wood to last for a week.

Two days later when the wind stopped, all the hired men left before dawn and sat impatiently over their nets until there was enough light for them to see. The storm had brought them fish. Every net sagged with the weight of the catch, but the pickerel were gone. Sunfish clogged the nets. Many were as small as a man's hand, all head and spine, and were completely worthless. Doggedly, the men worked until it was too dark to see. The nets were so laden that they couldn't even be pulled into the boats and taken to shore. Their arms and backs aching, their hands raw with puncture wounds from the spines, the men came to supper so exhausted they could hardly eat.

Elliot had spent the day leisurely bagging his nets so they could be set in shallow water.

That evening when Valdi and Runa were alone, Elliot knocked on the door. "I need a package of tobacco and a pen-knife," he said. "I'll set tomorrow."

Valdi brought both items and put them on Elliot's bill. When the door was shut, he said, mimicking Elliot's voice. "He'll set tomorrow. That is," he added sarcastically, "if he doesn't decide to spend all his time doing chores for you."

For the next four days, the hired men did nothing but clear sunfish from their nets. With the return of calm weather, unseasonably warm temperatures set in and with them, all sign of fish disappeared. Everyone came back empty-handed except Elliot. He always caught fish, sometimes as much as half a box to a net. The resentment felt over the sunfish turned to bitterness.

One night after Elliot had left with a package of Export makings and a key chain, Harold said to the others. "You know what he does with that stuff? I watched him with my binoculars."

His narrow lips were angrily clamped shut and his chin was thrust out. "He throws them into the water, that's what." When he saw they were skeptical, he became annoyed and his voice rose sharply.

"I'm telling you. I saw him. He sits in the bow, studying the water, then throws whatever he's got and sprinkles out the tobacco. If you don't believe me, then you explain what he wants with tobacco when he doesn't smoke." He jabbed his finger at one, then another. "Have you seen him smoke? Have you?"

"So what?" Valdi asked. "He catches fish, doesn't he? Maybe you should try it."

"That's not all he's caught," Harold shot back. His feelings, already raw from returning day after day with a poor catch, were hurt by Valdi's comment. "He's made more than wages already. He caught himself a fish when he got you to hire him on shares. Every time he pulls a fish out, you're losing money." He laughed nastily. "Valdi Gudmundson being taken by an Indian. I never thought I'd see the day." Before Valdi had a chance to reply, Harold stamped out.

Valdi brooded. Harold's words had particularly hurt because Valdi had been thinking much the same thing himself. Until he had had his heart attack, he had regularly brought in more than twice as much as any of his hired men. Now, any real exertion nearly strangled him with pain.

"I'd like to fire that Indian," he confided to Runa, watching her from the corner of his eye to see if she showed any signs of caring. During his long convalescence, their lovemaking had virtually stopped. Certain of her unfulfilled desire, he was afraid of losing her. She shrugged indifferently. "But I can't. He's the only one making us any money." He swept his pale hand across the table as if sweeping away crumbs. "I've got to keep him."

During the next few days, he tried to think of some way to just pay Elliot wages, but everything he planned left Elliot free to go to the mounties or fish inspectors about the illegal nets. He was leaning morosely on the counter watching the lake when Harold, who had come in for a cup of coffee, said, "You'd beter watch that Indian. I think he's out for more than fish."

Before Valdi could ask for an explanation, Runa came in. She had been searching for dried heads of grass. During the winter, she made centrepieces, which she then sold in the spring to some gift shops in town.

Harold studied her disapprovingly, then said, "I guess I'd better be going. I've got some nets to repair. Not that it matters much when you don't have some witchery to help you."

"Wait a minute," Valdi replied, hurrying to get up. "I've got some things to do. I'll come along."

When they were out of Runa's hearing, Valdi demanded, "Is there something between that Indian and Runa?"

Harold shrugged. "I didn't say that, but she was gone a long time for such a little bit of grass." He saw that Valdi was furious so he quickly added, "Maybe it's nothing. Runa wouldn't have anything to do with him anyway."

When Valdi returned to the cookshack, he couldn't resist going to the counter to look at the grasses Runa was sorting. There was less than half a basketful.

"Didn't get much," he said, watching her closely. She was a good-looking girl. She was nicely rounded and had good legs. He plucked a piece of grass from the back of her sweater.

She twisted her head to see what he was doing. "Brush me off," she said. "Crawling around in the brush, everything sticks to you."

"Was it worth it?" he asked. He ran his hand over her back and realized that she didn't have on a brassiere. Running his hand up and down between her shoulder-blades excited him.

With a twitch of her shoulders, she pulled away. "Does it look like it?"

Valdi watched her closely after that, but saw nothing suspicious. Still, he was not satisfied. Afraid that he might be missing something, he began staying awake as long as he could to be sure Runa fell asleep before he did. Sometimes, he leaned over and peered closely into her face to be sure she wasn't faking. When he slept, he was so tense that the light thump of a squirrel landing on the roof was enough to wake him.

During the fishing season, the only regular visitor to the camp was the driver of the truck that picked up the fish and sometimes brought supplies. He was nineteen years old and had acne. One day, after he was finished loading, he gave Valdi a letter.

"That's for the Indian who works for you," he said. "You be sure he gets it."

Valdi held the envelope against the window, but he couldn't make out any words. The return address was the Correctional Services Branch of the Manitoba government.

"Do you know what it is?"

"I don't know if I'm supposed to say anything," the kid answered self-importantly and cracked a knuckle. "It might be confidential."

"He works for me, doesn't he? I guess I got a right to know."

The kid popped another knuckle. "He got in a fight and knifed some guy. He was in jail for a year but they let him out on parole because he was going loony. He couldn't stand being locked up. He tried to kill himself. That's to tell him to check back in with his parole officer at the end of the season."

When Elliot came off the lake, Valdi met him outside the cookshack and gave him the letter.

"You knifed somebody, I heard."

"He started it," Elliot replied.

"How come they put you in jail then?"

Elliot walked away. Valdi, emboldened by Elliot's retreat, pressed close behind him. "How come?" he demanded.

Elliot turned on him. His dark face, normally so expressionless, was filled with hatred. He made a sharp, threatening motion with his left hand and Valdi instinctively stepped back.

"He was a white man," Elliot spat out. "In Manitoba, who ever believes an Indian?"

When Elliot was gone, the door shut behind him, a sense of relief swept through Valdi.

The next day when Elliot was on the lake, Valdi went into the storage shed. There wasn't much to see. In the cleared space there was an iron cot, a bedroll, a suitcase and an empty Coke bottle. Valdi searched the suitcase but found only extra clothing. What he had hoped to find were the receipts that Elliot had for the fish he had caught. Without them, he couldn't prove how much Valdi owed him.

He returned to the kitchen but could not concentrate on his game of solitaire. Throwing down the cards, he said, "$500. You could use some of it for new clothes. You haven't had anything new in a long time." He rubbed his hand over his mouth. "He watches you all the time. Did you know that?"

"They all watch me," Runa replied indifferently. She scattered flour across the counter and began rolling out dough for crusts. The morning sun glistened on the light, golden hair that covered the backs of her arms.

He cleared his throat. "Say you played up to him a little."

She quit rolling dough and stood absolutely still. Before the silence could stretch out, he quickly added, "Just say he did try something. Not much. Anything would do. And you yelled rape. There'd be lots of witnesses."

He saw she was annoyed, but he refused to give up. "He wouldn't get to do anything, you know. I'd be close by."

"So the mounties arrest him and they collect his wages. Or his parole officer does. Good thinking," Runa said, her voice tight.

"No, no. Say he got away. Accidentally. He'd run as far as he could and never come back."

"No," she replied vehemently.

"Why not? We've got nothing to lose."

"I don't want any part of it. We'll get by."

"It's $500," he insisted. He lowered his voice. "$500. That would carry us until winter fishing starts. I've got those nets to pay for, too, you know."

That evening, Runa tried to stay as far away from Elliot as possible, but Valdi glared at her until she moved closer to him. With the other men watching, the most she could do was lean close to put his dessert on the table.

When the men were gone, Valdi told her to go get something from the storage shed. She hurried into the storage shed, picked up a skein of wool and hurried out.

"Why didn't you yell?" Valdi demanded.

"He didn't do anything."

For the rest of the week, Runa refused to co-operate, but then, on the next Monday, when she was collecting an armload of wood, she overheard Valdi and Harold talking on the other side of the woodpile.

"I don't know," Harold was saying. "It's risky."

"$50. You should do it for nothing, the way you feel about him. It's got to look like an accident."

Not wanting to hear any more, Runa crept away.

An hour after supper, Runa took the water pail and went out, but instead of going to the shore, she put the pail down and entered the storage shed. Elliot was lying on his cot. She went to the back and pretended to search for something in the dark. In a minute, he joined her, holding up a lamp so she could see.

His face was smooth and his eyes seemed larger than ever. The muscles on either side of his neck stood out like taut ropes.

"What are you looking for?" he asked in his soft voice.

Runa ran her hand down the front of her blouse, pulling the buttons loose. Catching the material with both hands, she pulled it aside. She took his free hand and pulled him down. He rested the lamp on a sack of flour.

After that, he was urgent, demanding. It was over in five minutes. When he released her, she sat up and leaned against a pile of sacks. Neither one moved until they heard the cookshack door bang. As if on a signal, Runa screamed. Elliot was so startled that, at first, he simply stared. She screamed again.

"I'm coming," Valdi yelled. A voice from the direction of the bunkhouse wanted to know what was the matter.

Elliot sprang to his feet and bolted for the door. He crashed into Valdi and they both plunged off the steps. Elliot tried to pull free, but Valdi held his legs. He hit Valdi twice, just over the right eye and Valdi let go, but it was too late. Before Elliot could do more than stand, the hired men swarmed over him, pummelling him senseless. When he no longer moved, they stopped and left him curled on his side, his face in the dirt.

Runa came to the door and Valdi said, "What happened?"

Instead of replying, she ran past them to the cookhouse.

They carried Elliot inside and dumped him on his bed.

"We'll watch him," Harold volunteered. The knuckles of his left hand were badly scraped and he kept sucking at them to get out the dirt.

"No. I'll watch him." Harold was going to protest but Valdi silenced him by saying, "It was my wife." He clenched his fist suggestively. "He and I can talk about things while we wait."

Valdi took up his position in the doorway. After half an hour, he heard Elliot moving. He waited a while longer, then went around the far corner of the cookshack and waited. Elliot painfully let himself down the steps. His bedroll was over one shoulder and he carried his suitcase. He tried to run but his run was stumbling and, with each step, his body twisted in pain.

Valdi went into the cookhouse. Runa was knitting, her face rigidly set.

"You all right?" Valdi asked.

"Yes," she replied. She didn't look up.

"I didn't think you'd do it. I thought maybe you liked him." She continued to knit. "You didn't though, did you?" he said with satisfaction.

In the morning, over breakfast, he told the others that he had fallen asleep and that Elliot had run away. He gave them all $10 for their help. He gave Harold the $50 to lift Elliot's nets.

When the men were gone, he sat at the corner of the table where the sunlight warmed him. Half an hour went by, then Runa said, "There's a boat coming. It looks like Harold's."

Valdi pushed himself to his feet and hurried to the dock. Harold pulled alongside and, in his excitement, didn't even bother to tie up. Instead, he grabbed a net and held it over his head.

"The big mesh is okay," he shouted, "but look." The net had been cut to pieces. Even the cork and lead lines were beyond repair.

Unable to comprehend what had happened, Valdi grabbed the net and said, "Someone ran through it with their boat."

"No, it was that Indian. They're all like this."

Valdi kept feeling the net, rubbing the shredded parts between his fingers. "I'll call the mounties," he said, his voice still weak and ineffectual with shock. He pulled at the net and a piece of mesh came loose. As if he was suddenly able to grasp the seriousness of what had happened, he shook the net and shouted at Harold's thin face, "I'll call the mounties. They'll put him in jail for ten years."

"You can't," Harold replied and his eyes slid from Valdi's face to the tattered net.

Valdi held the net close and pulled at it so fiercely that he might have been trying to make each small square larger, but the nylon would not stretch. Instead, it cut cruelly into the soft, white flesh of his hands.

From the doorstep of the cookhouse, Runa watched her husband climb into Harold's boat and in half an hour, when she came back out, he and the boat were only a dark speck bobbing in the distance. She lifted a suitcase with each hand, and, without a backward glance, started down the dark ruts that led to the gravel highway south.

CAPITAL

Abel Shizter only came to town when opportunity knocked or necessity drove him. Today, though he would have vigorously denied it if anyone had asked, opportunity was knocking. Because he also had some grocery shopping to do, he went to the store first to get it over with. He didn't like spending money on groceries and though he only bought what his wife couldn't wrest from the rocky soil of his farm, he still entered the store with a grudging, sideways slant as if he was entering an area fraught with hidden danger.

As the prices were rung up with a thump and bang, he wondered out loud how everything could cost so much and mumbled Biblical quotations about usury and charity into the silences between the metallic ringing of the cash register. The silences were extended, sometimes lasting half a minute as Steini Storekeeper near-sightedly fumbled an item about in search of the price.

All the time Steini struggled with the groceries, Shizter hovered over him, a gaunt spectre enveloped in a khaki army-surplus coat that hung like a tent from his narrow shoulders. His thin, sharp face was so brown it might have been cured in a smokehouse. A purple bulge rose on the corner of his lower lip like a grape.

He kept his purse crushed in the bottom of his left pocket until the total was rung up, then he reluctantly drew it out and, still more reluctantly, counted out faded dollar bills as soft as worn cotton. As he counted them, he rubbed each one between his dirty thumb and forefinger. Laying one bill on another, he kept a glittering stare fixed on Steini's face but Steini never noticed. Intent on the money, he was bent so far over he might have been prostrating himself before a god. As he tried to keep track of the growing total, his watery blue eyes screwed themselves up until his entire face was twisted and warped.

Mrs. Steini Storekeeper—she had a name of her own once but it had long since been lost somewhere in the dark trenches formed by endless piles of canned goods—a square, jut-jawed woman who had spent her life guarding the vanilla extract and the penny candy, stood directly behind her husband. Nothing impressed or intimidated her. Not since she had been a young woman had she been known to trust anyone enough to begin bagging groceries before his name was signed on the bill or every cent placed on the counter.

At $10.12, Shizter's bony fingers reached into his purse only to come out empty. "I'm 85¢ short," he declared. Before he could say anymore, Mrs. Steini deftly pushed 2¢ back with her left hand while she snatched up a pound of coffee with her right.

"I'll pay you next time," he promised.

Ignoring him, she began to pack groceries into a cardboard box.

"You can't expect me to go without my coffee!"

Mrs. Steini finished, then tilted up her broad, square face with its frame of frizzled grey hair so that she was staring directly into Shizter's outraged eyes. She shoved forward her cupped hand. "You've owed $76.53 since last August the sixteenth." She didn't need to look at the receipt book.

Angrily, he stalked out. From behind the rack of potato chips, Billy Boy, his twelve-year-old son and diminished replica of himself, appeared, his thin lips suspiciously flecked with salt. He braced the box of groceries against his chest and staggered outdoors. Mrs. Steini put the coffee back on the shelf.

Shizter stood, body taut as a piece of stretched barbed wire, his head pulled stiffly back. With his hands braced on his hips and his long coat blowing about him, he might have been a survivor of some unsuccessful military campaign. His ears stood out from the side of his head, and his black hair hung over his collar in a ragged line.

The sky was clear and bright and a stranger used to a milder climate would have expected it to be summer, but the snow had just gone and, although there had been one rain, the air was still bitter. The wind ran up the river, leaped over the bank, swept through the stunted maple trees and filled every nook and cranny. When Billy Boy had managed to lift the groceries into the back of the truck, Shizter, his galoshes flopping like miniature black wings, started across the street. Billy Boy ran behind, carrying four empty one-gallon Javex bottles.

In front of the Main Street garage, Abel stopped beside a car and, after looking in the window, circled it three times, tried the doors, lifted the hood and, crouching, probed the caked dirt with his fingers. Satisfied, he went inside. Showing just above the top of a battered roll-top desk was a bald, freckled head.

"Got a '49 Ford out there, Norman," he said, pushing a piece of tobacco into the corner of his mouth.

"Spit in the can, not on the floor," Norman replied.

"Not much of a car. '49. It's a wonder you didn't haul it to the junkyard right off. Who abandoned it?"

Tires were piled in front of the picture-window. At one time, when expectations were high, Norman had planned on having a display room for new cars but that was before the promised highway had bypassed the town. Shizter pulled his coat around his knees and sat on the tires. Billy Boy was already using a tin cup to skim the oil barrel. He worked carefully so as not to stir up sediment.

"Steering's probably shot. More than likely got a cracked block. You want to give me $5, I've got my truck and I can haul it away." When there was no reply, he peered out the window. "Rubber's not bad. Some dumb kid might give $5 apiece for those tires."

"$75," Norman shouted from behind the desk. "As is." The top of his head was pink from the strain of trying to remember what the figures meant that he had written on old envelopes and business cards and lunch bags.

Shizter went outside and started the car. The radio worked and the upholstery was untorn but there was a knock in the motor.

"I wouldn't want to run it more than five mph," Shizter announced as he slid through the door. Billy Boy was lugging two full Javex bottles to the truck.

"I'm trying to balance my books," Norman shouted with barely controlled rage.

"$40."

"$50!" The veins on his head swelled until they formed a ridged, purple map. "$50, and get out of my hair."

Shizter drew a purse out of his right pocket. He counted out five $10 bills and laid them on top of the desk. The transaction took only a few minutes. "Damn Steini's wife anyway," he complained resentfully. "I was short 85¢ today on my groceries and she took back my coffee. She's a tight-fisted old bitch."

"Why didn't you pay her out of this?" Norman asked, jerking his thumb at the purse.

Quickly, Shizter stuffed the purse out of sight. "That's my capital," he replied indignantly.

They chained the car behind the truck. With Billy Boy at the wheel of the car, Shizter towed it out of town. He had to drive carefully. The brakes on the car only worked after they had been pumped three or four times and then, when they did catch, they jerked the car violently to the right.

Shizter's unpainted frame house was surrounded by crankshafts, motors and worn-out tires. A grey-and-white horse and five goats wandered aimlessly through the debris, browsing on the weeds. Shizter pulled up at the rear door of the house and while Billy Boy sat on the steps, straining the oil through a piece of flannelette sheet, Shizter washed the outside of the car with a mop. When the car was clean, he began to fill all the rusted spots with putty. It took him two hours, for the body of the car was badly pitted. That done, he made certain the radio worked properly. Next, he began to prepare the inside. He swept it, stapled white and red pom-pom trim along the top of the windows and hung two large foam dice and a kewpie doll from the rear-view mirror. Satisfied with the interior, he sprayed the grille with aluminum paint and the body with quick-drying black enamel.

The next morning, before he towed the car back to town, he sprayed fluorescent orange along the fenders and pasted red Christmas tape on the hood and trunk to make racing stripes. As they entered, the town was deserted but Shizter confidently parked the car at the front of the beer parlour. Against the grille he leaned a piece of cardboard with foot-high letters saying, "Hot Rod For Sale." Squatting on his heels, he began his vigil. Billy Boy crouched beside him, his back to the wind. Unmoving, they might have been two brown hawks dozing.

"Nobody's coming," Billy Boy said, picking up a twig and poking at his gap teeth. Like his father, his brow was high and bulging and his nose long. Neither of them had much chin.

"They'll come," his father replied, helping himself to a pork-and-raw-onion sandwich from the grocery bag beside him. "They always do. If you want to get ahead, you got to learn to be patient. The man that's willing to make everything ready and then wait, he gets what he wants."

All at once, Shizter spat violently into the street. Mrs. Steini was rushing back to the store from the post office. "God Almighty," he said. "You'd think it couldn't exist without her." He couldn't understand how her husband tolerated her. He preferred his own wife, a thin, yellow woman who moved like a fading shadow through the rooms of his house.

"She's like an overfed hen," he continued. "I wouldn't give a nickel a pound for her. She's got mean hands." His eyes tracked her until she disappeared inside the store.

He rested his back against the car bumper. "When she first came," he started, then stopped.

"What about when she first came?" Billy Boy asked eagerly, quick to scent past secrets.

"We was different. Times changed us," his father snapped, cutting off the conversation.

The hotel before which they sat was the only prosperous building on the street. Square, two stories high, it was a stucco cube with two front windows and a glass door. The windows were covered with venetian blinds that were always down. The street on which the hotel fronted was gravelled every fall but every spring the gravel sank from sight and ruts a foot or more deep formed and filled with water.

On either side of this muddy track, there were more empty lots than buildings. Besides the hotel, there was a café with a pool table and one pinball machine, a post office, the garage and a curling rink. Set back nearly half a block was a yellow-brick school and even farther behind that, so that it perched precariously on the river bank, was a clapboard church with a leaky roof. At one time, when the flat, silver surface of the river was used for a highway, the church had stood at the centre of the town but now it marked the decaying edge.

"It's not eleven o'clock yet," Shizter said, squinting at the sun. "They've got to get paid and that takes time and then they've got to get from there to here and most of them don't own a car."

"How'd you know they're to get paid?"

"I know'd. The cheques come three days ago."

Shizter was waiting for the Indians who had been cutting pulp that winter. Some of them had cut over 40 cords but there had been a delay in their getting their cheques. At $6.50 a cord some of them had big money coming.

In the distance, there was the rumble of a motor. A minute later, a truck rocked along the ruts and jolted to a stop in front of the café. Four passengers were jammed into the cab and another eight were clustered in the back with a piece of canvas pulled over their heads to protect them from clods of mud kicked up by the wheels. Two cars careened into the space beside them. Out on the street, the Indians shifted like sandpipers about to fly, then all together whirled into the café.

Shizter knew they were watching him from the café window but he paid no attention. Another car pulled up and in a minute the faces behind the glass multiplied. There was a brief flurry as one car filled again and was driven to the side door of the hotel. The passengers went inside and returned in a few minutes with a case of beer each. Shizter cleaned his nails with his pocket knife. Gradually, the Indians in the café trickled onto the sidewalk and stood behind their vehicles.

Standing up slowly, Shizter stretched and yawned, then meandered into the hotel. Billy Boy trailed behind him. There was no-one at the desk. The owner and his wife were shining up the parlour in anticipation of profit. Shizter eased up to the venetian blind and, like a sniper waiting for an enemy to expose himself, peeked through the slits. At first, nothing happened. The group of Indians merely studied the car more openly. Five minutes passed. At last, two young boys with their black hair greased back, wearing black leather jackets, blue jeans and cowboy boots, pigeon-toed their way across the street. As they reached the car, Billy Boy darted for the door. Shizter caught him by the collar and silently drew him back.

The two boys circled the car, their hands in their jacket pockets. The tallest one had on a red, embroidered shirt and a string tie. The shorter boy had a broad face and wore a white captain's hat heavy with gold braid. They leaned in the window to fondle the steering wheel. Quick as a swooping hawk, Shizter sped outdoors. The two boys started at the sight of him.

"Go ahead, go ahead," he said soothingly, pausing in midstride and lifting both hands palm outward. "That's why it's here, to give someone who wants a fine-looking car a chance to try it out. It's as nice a car as you're going to find."

"How much?" the boy with the embroidered shirt asked.

"Don't worry about it. No use talking price until you're sure you want it." Waving his hands about he herded the second boy around the car. "What's your name?" he asked once he had him safely settled.

"Orville. Orville Dejarlis."

"And yours?"

"Raymond Barrow," the boy with the captain's cap replied with a start. He had been admiring himself in the mirror.

"Pleased to meet you," Shizter responded with a quick smile.

The two boys were sneaking glances at the crowd on the sidewalk and, especially, at the cluster of girls who were watching the car with wide-eyed admiration.

"This is," Shizter announced, his voice rising to emphasize the importance of what he was going to say, "as fine a car as was ever made. Solid!" On the last word, he slapped the flat of his hand on the fender, being careful, at the same time, not to hit any putty. "Just listen to this radio." He leaned in and switched on the radio. "You can always tell a good car by the tone of the radio. Poor radios are a signal that you're getting a poor car. They might be able to disguise a poor motor or transmission because we're not all mechanics but the radio always gives them away. Did you ever hear of a Cadillac with a poor radio? I always say a good radio matters because even if something unexpected happened and you couldn't drive the car, you could still sit in it and listen to any station you wanted and it would still feel like you were going somewhere. Besides that, it would save you gas. Ain't that right, Billy Boy?"

"Yes, sir!"

Billy Boy was hanging onto the back of the front seat. He liked to get as close to a radio as possible. When his father was away, he would turn on one of their seven radios to full volume and sit with his ear pressed right against it, beating his foot on the floor and grinning like a fool. He kept a broom in one hand in case his mother tried to bother him. Sometimes, he couldn't hear anything for an hour afterward.

"Another thing that matters is the way a car looks." He reached up and tickled the fringe. "Ain't them pom poms fine, Billy Boy?"

"Yes, sir."

One of Billy Boy's first lessons in salesmanship and his prime function, besides fetching and carrying, was saying yes to whatever was asked. His father felt it put his customers in the right frame of mind. Hearing *no* confused them as to what they wanted.

Unused to so much attention, Raymond squirmed with embarrassment. Before he could get out of the car, Shizter slammed the door shut and scrambled into the back.

"Take it down the street," he instructed. "Just nice and easy. It doesn't cost anything to try it."

Raymond shot a glance to where the girls were watching him expectantly. He turned on the key. Right away, Shizter leaned over the seat and turned the radio up until it was loud enough to disguise the knock. As the car went past, all the girls giggled and waved. Orville waved back. They reached the end of the block, made a U-turn and returned. The girls all waved again.

When they had stopped and the radio was turned off, Shizter said, "There was a lot of snow last winter." Though the ride was over, Raymond was still holding onto the wheel. "Couldn't have cut much pulp, I guess. I don't think anybody was able to cut more than fifteen cords."

"I cut twenty," Orville corrected. "And Raymond, he did better. He cut 30."

Shizter let the information slide by as of no importance. He pulled up the sleeve of his coat, studied his watch and then leaned out the window to stare down the road.

"Go see if that fellow who said he was going to buy this car is coming," he said to Billy Boy.

To the other two he explained, "Young fellow said he wanted this car but he had to go to Winnipeg to get his money. Got a ride on the transfer and going to hitch-hike back." He watched Raymond's face droop with disappointment. "I told him that he might be too late, though. When all you want for a car like this is $175, you can't expect it not to be snapped up. I'm even throwing in a gallon of high-grade oil."

He picked a Javex bottle off the floor and opened it. Wrestling it around, he said, "Sniff that." Both boys sniffed. "That's enough oil for the next three months. All you've got to buy is gas."

Raymond said he would take the car. They signed the papers, then Shizter went to Steini's store and flinging open the door, swaggered up to the counter without giving Mrs. Steini a glance and slapped Raymond's cheque onto the counter.

Steini picked up the cheque but before he could read it, his wife snatched it from his hands. She studied every letter and number, turning it over twice.

"I come to pay my bill," Shizter announced, "and from now on, I'll take my business elsewhere. Just give me a receipt for my bill, saying paid in full."

Mrs. Steini eyed him warily. "We don't take two-party cheques. Never have. You know that's our policy."

"Is it?" Shizter asked.

She looked at the cheque again, then at the box that contained the unpaid accounts. She leaned toward it as if ready to give in.

"It's good," Shizter announced. "There's nothing wrong with that cheque. I guarantee it. I just got it for selling a car." He knew that she never missed anything that happened on Main Street. As they talked, they could hear a car motor racing, then gears clashing as the Ford went racing by.

"Good as gold," he repeated, obviously restraining a smile.

Mrs. Steini put down the cheque and folded her arms over her ample chest. "We don't take two-party cheques."

Quickly, Shizter plucked up the piece of paper. "All right, all right," he cried in an offended voice, "if that's the way you feel, I'll cash it myself and bring you the money."

Mrs. Steini looked unsure of herself. Her eyes were anguished. She had worried over Shizter's account for a year and was desperate for it to be paid. "Maybe," she said, "we could make an exception just this time."

"No. No. Absolutely not." Shizter shoved the cheque into his pocket and drew himself up. "I wouldn't want you to take the chance that the cheque was no good. Billy Boy, you might as well get two pounds of drip coffee and a pound of sugar lumps. We'll pay for everything at once."

Mrs. Steini wrote up the bill so slowly that she seemed to grudge each letter, then presented it to be signed. Shizter carelessly initialed it.

Outside, as the '49 Ford rocketed past him, its wheels jerking so wildly in the ruts that they seemed ready to fly in all directions, Shizter counted five dark faces in the front seat, seven in the back. As he drove away, he could see Mrs. Steini's face pressed close to the window.

The pulp mill had a temporary office at the edge of town. Shizter went there, cashed the cheque and counted his money twice. From the direction of Main Street, he heard a sharp bang.

He drove back to the crossroads. Sitting up straight as a dignitary in a parade, he paused to look down the street. To the left, the Ford was stopped in the middle of the street. The hood was up and the owner was standing, his shoulders drooping, looking at the motor.

"Thrown rod, most likely," Shizter commented, nudging the wheel to the right.

"Aren't you going to pay Mrs. Steini?" Billy Boy asked. The sugar and the two pounds of coffee were wedged between them.

"Pay her!" Shizter exclaimed. "Pay her! With what? I don't have any living money." He grabbed at his pocket to reassure himself his purse was safe. "This is my capital." He wrenched the wheel around and pressed on the accelerator. A hail of mud flew backward toward the town.

"You want to get along in this world, Billy Boy," he insisted sternly, "you'd better learn a lesson." Ducking his head, he spat out the window and surveyed an old car sitting in a farmyard. "If you don't look after your own capital, nobody else will."

A PRIVATE COMEDY

Behind the Greek café, surrounded by six-foot high rows of soft-drink cases, Hermann Finnson and Albert Snifeld were eating chocolate ice-cream cones.

Without warning, Darlene Melouish appeared. She had just started working as a waitress at the café. Her white uniform was starched and stiff looking with her name embroidered in red over her right breast.

"Hi! How are you?" she said.

Startled, they both jerked around to stare. They had never before met anyone at the back door of the Greek's. After his first moment of shock, Hermann, his face wreathed in a flowing black beard and long black hair, sat silent and unmoving. He was dressed in a blue suit jacket with the buttons torn off, a faded red checkered shirt and olive-drab pants. Albert, leaning his oval body forward, his chocolate-rimmed mouth sagging open, eyed the intruder suspiciously.

The soft-drink cases formed the shape of a horseshoe with a piece taken out of the back. The enclosed ground was littered with garbage. A primitive sidewalk had been made by laying down a row of boards that had become barely distinguishable from the mud.

Darlene's forehead was too broad and her mouth too wide for her to be pretty but she was not unattractive. Her blond hair had been cut short at the sides and left long at the back and her eyes were the light brown of young hazelnuts. She stood pensively for a long moment as if preparing to say something important but then, with a quick movement, skipped up the stairs and disappeared behind the green kitchen door.

Hermann was upset. Ever since both his legs had been amputated close to the thigh, he had hated to be seen by anyone. The only time he came uptown was at ten o'clock on Sunday morning when the rest of the town was asleep or at church. Albert brought him, hurrying from back lane to back lane with his rolling, stiff-legged shuffle, on a small wooden platform set on four tricycle wheels. Their coming was a ritual. Hermann always took his time about drawing out his leather purse and counting out four dimes. Albert took them to the door. The change was taken and in a few minutes two double-decker ice-cream cones were thrust into his waiting hands.

When they came the next Sunday, it was Darlene who brought the cones. Instead of just reaching them out, she presented one to Albert and one to Hermann as formally as if they had been customers sitting at the tables inside. She had on false eyelashes that kept making her blink and her eyelids were bright green.

"How are you today?" she asked and paused for an answer.

Albert thought she was making fun of them. His face darkened and he raised his fist menacingly.

Sharply, Hermann reprimanded him. "No, stop it. Bad, Albert. Bad."

To Hermann's relief, Albert lowered his fist. He still thrust his face forward with the belligerence of an angry child. His face was smooth with flat unobtrusive features. His ears were like small shells.

Darlene looked frightened. Afraid that she might complain to the mounties about the incident, Hermann tried to reasure her. "Albert's all right. He works for me as a blacksmith. He didn't mean any harm. It's just that he thought you were making fun of him. Some people do." Hermann couldn't keep the worry out of his voice. Without Albert, he was helpless.

Albert was 25 but he had the barrel-shaped body of a small child. He had no discernible hips or waist and so little neck that his round head seemed to balance precariously on his shoulders like a large, smooth boulder.

Sympathetically, Darlene said, "It's all right. The next time he comes, I'll give him extra big scoops."

Talking to Darlene had been painful for Hermann. Except for the briefest possible conversations when someone was ordering metal work, he never spoke to anyone but Albert and to him he merely gave orders. Two years before, when he had come home from the hospital, he had driven away anyone who had come to see him. He was not going to be a free freak show for anyone. He refused to have a mirror in his house.

During the next week, in spite of his efforts to shove her out of his mind, Darlene's smile and her hair and her long legs disappearing under the hem of her uniform crept into his thoughts. The next Sunday, he found excuses not to go to the café. The break in their routine left Albert bewildered. Time and again he came to point in the direction of the café and make the deep, guttural noise that did him for speech. After the sixth time, Hermann lost his temper and yelled at him. Albert ran into his bedroom. Whenever Albert got his feelings hurt, he always went into his bedroom and sat facing the wall and sulked until he forgot why he was there. Fortunately, he had a short memory.

Hermann forced himself to concentrate on a sketch of a wrought-iron gate. On warm summer days, he worked on his back porch. He didn't mind if people saw him then, for when he was in a chair behind his desk no-one could tell that anything was wrong with him. He was broad shouldered and deep chested. When he rolled up his sleeves, his arms were corded with muscle.

Under supervision, Albert could do the actual blacksmithing but Hermann had to plan everything so that each job was as simple as possible. A flock of gulls had been sitting on the road. All at once, they rose into the air. Looking up, Hermann saw Darlene approaching.

Overcome with panic, he called in a harsh whisper, "Albert! Albert! Come and help me. I want to go in."

Albert stayed in his bedroom.

Hermann didn't dare to try to climb down to his wheeled platform by himself. He had attempted it once and the platform had slipped from beneath him, pitching him ignominiously to the ground where he had flopped about like a stranded carp.

Unable to escape, he bent close to his desk. He was going to pretend he didn't know Darlene was there but she thrust a melting ice-cream cone between his face and the paper on which he was working. To keep it from dripping on his sketch, he snatched the cone away and sat back. Darlene was wearing a skimpy white beach jacket decorated with red hearts. Inside each heart were the words, "Love me." On her head she wore an outrageously large straw hat. Tiny blue pom poms hung from its brim.

Hearing her voice, Albert couldn't resist coming to peek around the corner of the doorway. She reached the second cone to him.

"You didn't come," she explained, "and I was going swimming so I thought I'd bring your cones." Chocolate had trailed down her hands. She licked it off.

With a jab of annoyance, Hermann extracted his change purse from his shirt pocket. He pried open the snaps with his thumb, plucked out 40¢ and held it out to her. She dropped the change into her jacket pocket. Her hands, he noticed, were slender and delicate. His were dark and calloused.

"You're all right, aren't you?" she asked.

"We're okay," he replied, licking the ice cream to keep it from trickling down his arm. He tried to keep his eyes focused on a middle distance but her jacket kept swinging open to reveal that she was wearing nothing but a white tassled bikini.

"I'm Darlene," she said.

Reluctantly, as if he was being forced to give up a carefully guarded secret, he admitted, "I'm Hermann. That's Albert."

Albert ignored them. He was sitting on the edge of the wooden sidewalk, his close-cropped head bent greedily over his cone.

"You've got a lot of good stuff here," she observed, surveying the yard.

Hermann's house sat by itself on a narrow strip of ground that lay between the gravel road and the lake. It was a small, shingled building. When they had taken it over, it had been in poor condition but they had repaired it, insulating the walls by stapling layers of newspaper between the studs. By tearing down another shanty, they obtained enough lumber to face the inside walls. The building next to them they gutted and outfitted with blacksmithing equipment. They also built a board sidewalk between the house and the shop and then attached another sidewalk to one side so that Hermann could reach the road.

Since Hermann preferred not to be seen, they usually slept during the early part of the day and worked at night. When it was dark, they laboured over their forge, hammering iron for the farmers and fishermen of the area. During the winter, steam and light poured from the frame building in such quantities that, at times, they seemed to be working within the centre of the fire itself. In the summer, they did less blacksmithing and frequently spent warm summer nights searching the back lanes for anything that might be of value.

At such times, Albert didn't tow Hermann. Because his hands wouldn't reach the ground, Hermann pushed himself along with two pieces of hockey-stick handle that he had tipped with rubber. As they scurried through the town, always ready to duck into the deepest shadows if a car appeared, Hermann's arms worked like pistons and Albert trailed behind, waddling along, his stomach thrust forward, a burlap sack over his shoulder. Each time Hermann rooted out an object worth keeping, Albert grabbed it up and shoved it into the sack. Sometimes, when there was a chance of their getting something large, Albert pulled a wagon.

As a result of their forays, they had gradually taken over more and more of the grassy space around the house until now Darlene gazed upon half an acre covered with stacks of beer bottles in disintegrating cardboard boxes, rusting bed springs, leaky radiators and assorted pieces of furniture. One pile was made up exclusively of radios that didn't work.

"Yes," Hermann replied, "we've got lots of things." He smiled and scanned the yard with a pleased sense of possession.

Darlene waited for him to say something more and, when he did not, she left. Hermann felt a sense of relief, but that evening he was unable to work. Instead, he went out by himself and spent until four in the morning racing erratically up and down the town's back lanes. He collected nothing and finally returned home after nearly being run over by a car.

On Tuesday evening Darlene returned. Hermann watched her while pretending not to, but Albert wasn't so circumspect. As she drew nearer, Albert jumped to his feet and began to jig excitedly. She veered to join them, Albert ducking his head from side to side to see if she had anything in her hands. She rummaged in her purse and brought out an O'Henry. He tore off the wrapper and stuffed the entire bar into his mouth.

"He enjoys treats," she said.

"He's a good boy," Hermann replied, watching Albert trying to chew, "but he likes sweets too much."

She hesitated, avoiding his eyes, then, in a rush, said, "I hope you don't mind me coming. I wanted to go for a walk but it's no fun if you've got no place to go."

The honesty of her statement checked the sarcastic remark he had been going to make. Disarmed, he fell silent and she took his silence for acceptance.

While he was in the hospital, checkers had become an

obsession with him. Since coming home, however, he had played only against himself. His checkerboard was made from a piece of white paper. He had drawn the squares with red and black crayons. His markers were Coca Cola and 7-Up bottle caps.

"I haven't played checkers for a long time, not since grade eight," Darlene said wistfully. "I was never smart enough for anyone to want to play with me."

Before he could reply, a harsh blast from the direction of the harbour made them look up. A white cruise-ship was leaving. The dresses of the women who lined the rails were bright daubs of colour.

Hermann swept the bottle caps into a pile, then began setting them on their squares.

Darlene competed innocently, without planning any of her moves. At first, Hermann played sullenly but, after awhile, her childlike glee at jumping one of his men and her expressions of dismay at his jumping two or three of hers made him amused. While they played, he watched to see if she would find excuses to look under the table at his stumps. The backs of her arms, he noticed, were lightly covered with blond hair that glistened in the sun.

He won the first two games easily. Her strategy consisted of moving directly ahead so that he was forced to jump. That way she always got some of his men. The third time, by playing with great care, he was able to let her win without being obvious about it.

"I had an accident," he said suddenly.

"I thought so," she answered.

"Don't you want to know about it?"

She shook her head and studied the board. There was no secret about her strategy. When she was planning a move, she traced each shift or jump with her index finger.

"Haven't you asked at the café about me?"

She shook her head again. His question had made her lose track of the move she had worked out.

"Why not?" he asked resentfully. "Everybody's interested

in cripples."

She shrugged. "We're all cripples, I guess. On some it shows more than others. One of our neighbour's boys fell out of a tree on his head. Couldn't see anything except a little cut, but now they have to tie him in a chair so he can sit up."

Her answer so rattled him that he played the next game in defeated silence.

When she was gone, Hermann said to Albert, "I don't want her back again. If she comes, you chase her off." But that night after Albert was sleeping, Hermann dragged a suitcase from under his bed. He unlocked it and from under a pile of personal belongings including his good suit that he intended to be buried in, extracted a mirror, which he hung from a nail. He studied his image for half an hour before taking a pair of scissors from the table and trimming his beard and hair.

For the next month Darlene came twice a week. Albert watched for her every evening and as soon as she rounded the corner, instead of chasing her off, he danced about so that his round body bobbed like a child's inflatable toy, weighted at one end. Darlene always brought him a treat. Usually, it was something from the kitchen for which she didn't have to pay—a bag of french fries or a hamburger or hot dog that had been left over.

The first week in August was warm and still, perfect weather for sitting on the porch and playing checkers, but Darlene didn't come. Hermann and Albert watched for her every evening. On the third night Hermann pushed himself downtown and secreted himself behind some trucks on the moving-company lot across from the café. From there, he watched for a glimpse of her in the windows. All week he slept very little and, when he should have been working, he found himself sitting on the porch, staring down the road. Albert was no better. He would be making anchors and would suddenly put down his hammer and tongs and stand forlornly at the corner of the shed. Hermann gave up yelling at him for then Albert spent more time in his bedroom than he spent looking for Darlene.

They stayed home that Sunday and just after eleven Darlene appeared. She was pale and silent. Her smile was slack. Normally, she rattled on, telling him all the gossip she had heard at the café.

"You been fired?" he finally asked.

She bit her lip and he could see that she was forcing back tears.

"It's your move," she said.

He folded his arms. "Not until you tell me what's wrong."

"I think I'm pregnant."

"Who?" he asked, too shocked to say more.

"I don't know. I didn't have enough for rent so I had to work downstairs a few times." Tears trailed down her cheeks.

He had forgotten about the girls at the café working downstairs. There were two small rooms with pink walls and double beds. No-one was ever forced to work downstairs. There was no need. Wages were $6 and one meal a day. Fifteen minutes downstairs paid $10 and waitresses, like everyone else, had landlords and doctors to pay and groceries to buy.

"I didn't want to," Darlene said. She stopped to get her voice under control. In a helpless, bewildered tone, she added, "There were too many days in the week."

She sat awkwardly with her knees together and her feet toed in.

"I'll give you extra money," he said, his voice anguished.

She shook her head slowly as a tolling bell. "My parents lived on charity all their lives. I won't. You have to save yourself. Nobody can save you except yourself. I've found that out."

"You do it for strangers," he replied angrily. "Do it for me. I'll pay you." He was nearly shouting. He dragged a $10 bill from his pocket and threw it on the table between them.

A sudden breeze sent it whirling to the ground. Neither of them paid it any attention.

"I've got to go now," Darlene said.

That night he didn't leave his chair but sat, wrapped in a quilt, watching the orange moon perform its nightly miracle of rising from the purple water. It climbed until it was above him, then stopped and stared unblinking like the eye of some solemn god before beginning its long journey down. He slept and was awakened by the sun shining on his face.

In the early dawn, he shaved and trimmed his moustache until it was no wider than the lead of a pencil. When the drugstore opened, he was impatiently waiting outside. He bought a wheelchair and had Albert push him in it to the barber's. While Hermann had his hair cut, Albert collected groceries, a blue paper table-cloth, paper napkins, a set of blue melmac, a bottle of Gallo wine, a $25 engagement ring and two boxes of chocolates.

After preparing a roasting chicken and vegetables, Hermann washed and dressed. His skin had some of the fragile transparency it had developed through his long convalescence but he was still angularly handsome. His straight black hair was neatly combed. His eyes, with their dark pupils and long lashes, might have been a woman's. His blue, double-breasted suit was creased from being packed away so long but he sponged out most of the creases and carefully folded the legs and pinned them in place. He made Albert change his shirt before he sent him with a note asking Darlene to come for supper. Her printed YES was awkward and childish.

Hermann rehearsed the points of his speech to himself. He would tell her he had some money saved. He wouldn't tell her how much unless she asked but it was $900. He would mention that he could have a lot more business if he wanted it. He would even promise to buy artificial legs and learn to use them. That was what they had wanted him to do at the hospital. They could rent a proper house close by.

Albert could stay by himself but eat with them.

His agitation was so great that he had to move around. He pushed himself to the shop. Normally, the smell of coal and iron calmed him but now it had no effect. He pushed himself to the house, straightened everything on the table for the tenth time, looked into the oven, then returned to the porch to fidget with the buttons of his jacket.

He hefted the chocolates and wondered if he should have bought all soft centres. He wondered if she liked hard centres. His suit was a little out of style but he didn't think she would notice. His face was just like it was before the accident except for some lines that spread from the corners of his mouth and eyes. The pain had done that.

The house was so hot he could barely breathe, so he sat outside. Over the lake there were clouds that looked like piles of soft ice cream. Albert had quit work and was stretched out on a green-and-white lawn chair drinking an Orange Crush.

Hermann checked his watch again and wheeled himself to the shop. The block and tackle with its massive hook hung beside the forge. The links were large and black. He grabbed the hook and pulled on it until he was an inch off the wheelchair, then he eased himself down. Using his strength made him feel good. They hadn't been using the hook but he was glad they had kept it. They would need it if they took larger pieces of work. He would need to build up his business if he was to have a wife and child. He would have to get out and talk to people.

He intended to give her the ring after supper. Albert was going to the movie. The second box of chocolates was for him. When they were alone, he would ask her to marry him. Even though they could go to bed right away that night, they would not. They would wait. He had wrenched all thought of women from his mind while he was in the hospital but, now, her being close had made him face the situation again. If he was going to be her husband, he could not be a husband in name only.

He looked down the road and saw that it was empty. He felt a small sense of relief. His palms were slippery with sweat. Eddyville, he knew, was small enough that she was sure to have heard about what he had done today. Since she was coming that meant she was going to accept him. Suddenly, he felt frightened. He checked the road again.

He tried to visualize Darlene with her clothes off. He imagined her taking off her blouse, unzipping her skirt, but the image faded and he saw, instead, a picture of himself undressing. A pain like a hot coal seared his heart. Since his accident, he always tried to undress without looking at himself.

Darlene came around the corner of the post office and started down the road. He could see that she had on a white dress with a full skirt. In the distance, she could have been an angel. He watched her for a moment, then frantically wheeled himself into the shop.

Albert was asleep when Darlene reached the house. She tip-toed past him. No-one was in sight so she put the carton of grape soda and a box of Ritz crackers on the table. She knew that Hermann couldn't be far so she waited at the juncture of the two sidewalks. The setting sun was a nearly transparent scarlet ball that seemed to take up the entire sky.

One section of sidewalk ran before and behind her. The second lay at her right hand and her shadow, falling in a thin line across the ground, made an adjoining but thinner arm so that a cross which seemed to have once been broken was now repaired. She waited for nearly five minutes before going to check in the blacksmith shop.

When she opened the door, Hermann had his back to her. He had tied a rope to the hook beside the forge, made a noose, slipped it over his head and pushed himself out of his wheelchair. As she watched, his truncated body revolved slowly to the right but before he turned far enough for her to see his face, he stopped and began to revolve to the left.

THE NOVICE

He rose and fell violently but not as violently as he had in the boat. The boat, half empty because they had unloaded supplies at two camps, had been flung before the wind so that it crashed into successive walls of dark water until the timbers and steel had cried and groaned without stop. Now, clutching at cracks in the ruptured wood as desperately as at handholds on a high, sheer cliff, the first mate pressed himself to the piece of wreckage his thrashing arms had found in the darkness.

Spume from the crests of towering waves struck him as sharply as hail, forcing his eyes shut. To protect his face, he tried to pull himself against the wood while tucking his head into his chest but, immediately, a wave cascaded down upon him, engulfing him in a rush of sound, threatening to tear him loose from his precarious position. Unable to breathe, he automatically forced his head and shoulders up. His back arced into a tight bow as he struggled for air.

A second wave struck his upright body and the board that he had gripped with his left hand snapped in half. Terrified, he scrabbled for another handhold. As the fingers of his right hand were slipping, his flailing left hand caught an iron bar. He knew then that he was holding onto a piece of the forward cabin. Towel racks had recently been fitted over the wash-stands.

Darkness had engulfed them when the *Sally Anne* foundered. Her own weak lights were snuffed out and there was no light in the sky, not even the fitful lightning that normally flickered all summer long over the metal-rich eastern shore. This lightning sometimes turned dangerous but more often it licked its way along the clouds like a grass fire seen from a distance. Normally, the mate watched it with a wary eye for it seemed to him that the flickering light was a constant warning of barely contained violence. However, he now would have given a great deal for it to begin. Not only would it have pushed back the darkness but it would have marked the shore.

At first, choking and retching, he fought only to survive each wave. Then the wind stopped and as he lay motionless, his head tipped back, he worried about his ticket. He had hoped to be a captain and he wondered if the loss of the boat would cost him his chance. He did not think about it actively, for his mind was numbed by what had happened. The thought rose of its own accord and floated as aimlessly about his mind as he floated about the lake. As the shock started to wear off, he reached into the darkness, first with one arm, then the other. He found nothing. He waited, then as the noise of the water lessened, he called out, "Is anybody there?"

The darkness was thick, solid. He could see nothing and seeing nothing was sure that there was nothing.

"That you, Jess?" The voice was filled with sudden hope. Another voice and then another joined in.

"Wait a minute," the mate ordered in amazement. Relief that he was not alone surged through him. "Call off your names."

"Bob."

"Arni."

"Triggvi Johnson."

From the sound of the voices, the men all seemed to be clinging to the same piece of wreckage.

"Anyone else out there?" he shouted at the darkness. There was no reply. There had been nine crew members and one passenger. "What kind of condition are you in?"

"I think my arm is broken," Bob replied.

"Arni?"

"I'm okay."

"Triggvi?"

Triggvi was their passenger. He shouldn't have been with them. The *Sally Anne* was a freight boat. It wasn't built to carry passengers. He was with the Conservation Department and they had agreed to take him because his plane was grounded by the weather.

"Not so good." The words were forced. "Sitting at a government desk doesn't get you ready for this. But I'll make it," he added with sudden determination. "As soon as I get home, we're going to BC for the holidays. It's the first time I've got away in five years."

"Did anybody see the captain?"

There was silence. He had seen no-one himself. From the moment the boat went over, he was alone with the terror of being crushed by the water. He had never known that water could be so heavy. He remembered fighting savagely to get free of his rubber boots. All his childhood fears of being smothered had been realized then. Beneath the water, the noise had been incredible—the beating of the engine, the rending of wood, the flailing of his own limbs, all magnified.

Talking, although it comforted them, was too difficult to keep up. It took too much energy and interfered with their effort to stay attached to the wreckage. They couldn't lie on the wall for their combined weight would drive it under the surface, so they dangled from it like decorations from a chandelier, their bodies swaying limply with the waves. There was no point in trying to do more than wait for they had no idea in which direction safety lay.

The mate tried to visualize the other three but he could not. It was easiest to form a picture of Triggvi—round head, round body, small brown moustache—because he was a curiosity. The mate realized as he lay in the water, his arm wrapped around the iron bar, that he had no idea what Arni and Bob looked like. He had never cared for the crew. It was was not that he disliked them. When crews reassembled in the spring, they were gossiping every moment they were awake, asking about everyone with whom they had ever shipped. He had never been like that. When he had a question, it was about the boats.

"The water's not too cold," Triggvi said. He sounded frightened. The darkness was making him want to talk.

"We can be grateful for that all right," Arni agreed.

They would be cold enough by morning, the mate thought, but he said nothing. He wished the captain was with them. The captain would have known what to do. All he would have had to do was follow orders. The order by which he had governed his life would not have been broken and he would, dangling from the wreckage, still have been secure. Not having a captain any longer, he wished for a compass but their compass was gone.

He looked up. There were no stars, no moon, no sun. It had been a long time since he had charted a course by the heavens but he was not concerned. He would manage. He didn't even need a sextant. All he needed was for the direction of east and west to be revealed. If they swam in either of those directions, pushing the wreckage before them, they were sure to find land.

A wave swept under them, lifting them up, then the wreckage tipped and they slipped down into the next trough.

Just before the *Sally Anne* foundered, the mate had been in his bunk, but he knew approximately where they should be. They were no more than an hour out of the Narrows so they were in a stretch of water four miles wide.

What was working against them was that there was a strong northward current in the Narrows and if they didn't get to shore they would be pulled into an area where the lake was twenty miles across. Not that being ashore would necessarily save them. At most, it would give them a fighting chance. On both sides, the inhospitable shores were made up of sand bars and rock ledges interspersed with stretches of marsh.

Splintered wood was gnawing at the mate's arm. Earlier, he had tried to pull off his jacket but, unable to free the jammed zipper, he had given up. He was glad he hadn't got rid of the jacket. It was wool and even soaking wet, it helped to keep him warm. To keep it from being torn, he broke off some of the sharp splinters.

When he had turned over the watch to the captain, he had gone straight to his cabin. After wedging himself into his bunk so he wouldn't be pitched onto the floor by the violent motion of the boat, he had immediately fallen asleep. Later, he had wakened just as quickly when the engines changed their normal rhythm. He would never know what had happened to make the captain risk trying to turn around and run before the storm. He wondered if it was possible that, after all these years, the captain had suddenly lost faith in his own ability to weather the storm.

Feeling the ship heave to starboard, he had rolled out of the bunk, scrambled on his hands and knees to the door, forced it open and staggered to the rail. Before he could go any farther, a wave had engulfed him, knocking him off balance. The next wave, which struck less than a heartbeat later, tore him loose and swept him clear as the *Sally Anne* was driven under.

His arm ached so he shifted his hold on the iron bar. He found it hard to believe he was not in his bunk. He kept expecting to wake and feel the boat riding out the storm. His faith in the boat had been so overwhelming that he had to force himself to realize it had been destroyed.

He had always felt its intricacy would protect it. The complexity of its creation—it had to be conceived, constructed, nailed, bolted, welded, glued, all according to a carefully worked-out plan—seemed to guarantee its existence. The engine, the drive shaft, the propeller, the wheel, he had made these his study. He could draw them with precision, could recite their exact measurements. So strong was his faith that, as long as the lake was free of ice, he lived on the boat, never leaving it until the end of the shipping season. Throughout the winter, he lived alone in one room in an old house near the harbour, patiently waiting for the season to begin again. A day never passed when he didn't walk to the docks.

His security had also been fed by the boat's age. Not having seen its beginning, he had a blind faith it would go on forever. He felt this in spite of the swamp full of rotting derelicts beside the harbour.

He admitted that there had been signs of wear, signs that the boat also suffered from mortality—the motor faltered at times—but they had always fixed it. There had been leaks but they had been found and sealed. When they couldn't find all the leaks, they added extra pumps. Every spring as the boat sat in dry-dock, they had faithfully repainted it, coat on coat until it sat as white and majestic as a shrine.

"Arni," he called with a suddenness that startled even him.

"Here."

"Bob."

"Here."

"Triggvi."

There was no answer.

The deep troughs muffled the sound. "Did you hear anything?" he demanded of the other two.

They had heard nothing.

Fear tightened the muscle under the mate's jaw. Somewhere close, the moustached civil servant was dying, his short, round body turning endlessly with the shifting current. He wanted to cry out in protest but he knew it was no use. Nor would his plunging into the darkness do any good. His life, he realized, was as fragile as the gauze wings of the mayflies that rose from the lake each summer to spiral briefly toward heaven.

The first mate held his wrist close to his face so he could see the luminous dial of his watch. "It's just after midnight."

He knew what they were calculating. Dawn was to come at 4.37. With first light, they would be able to see just what they were hanging onto. He guessed it was most of one wall. Dawn would also reveal how far they were from safety.

He had never done anything except work on the boats. Grade ten finished with, he had signed on as a deck-hand. From that time on, he had given himself to a succession of boats until he had found the *Sally Anne*. Other men had other passions to disturb their lives. He never slept so well as when he was in his bunk, his ear tuned to the steady rhythm of the motor. Unlike the others, he had been careful not to encumber himself with a wife and children.

A quick swell of anger and disappointment swept through him. "I'm going to work around to Bob," he said. "Arni, you come around to the left until you catch up to me."

Painfully, with a left hand softened and robbed of feeling by the water, he fumbled for a new handhold, found a jagged edge and pulled himself awkwardly along. He told Arni about the iron rod, described the edge, tried to guide him. As the mate talked, he searched, found a bolt, crabbed sideways to what had been a porthole, then his fumbling hand caught Bob's shoulder.

Arni was slapping at the wood, moving around the perimeter of the wreckage like an angry dog. When he arrived, grumbling and complaining to himself, the mate ordered him to take off his belt and bind himself to the wreckage. When he was sure his order had been carried out, he turned his attention to Bob.

"How's your arm?"

"It's starting to hurt," Bob complained through gritted teeth. "I can feel the bone grinding close to my shoulder."

He undid Bob's suspenders and used them to tie him in place. Then he felt for the broken arm, caught it at the wrist and elbow and pushed it into the front of Bob's shirt so that it would be held in place. For the time being, it was the best he could do. Later, he would make a sling. He tied his own belt to a projecting two-by-four and slipped his arm through the loop.

"Where were you when it happened?" he asked.

"I was getting a cup of coffee."

"What about Cookee?" He and the cook had shipped

together for five years.

There was a pause as they tipped over the peak of a large wave and slid down its side in a rush of foam.

"He was standing behind the stove. Everything fell on him."

He tried not to think about that. He checked his watch. It still showed just after midnight. He was disappointed but not knowing the exact time didn't really matter. Dawn would come.

Close together, he reassured himself, they had a better chance of surviving than if each was alone. If one of them passed out, the others could keep his head out of the water. Until the next day began, all they could do was try to endure. The *wreckage*, he started to think and then it came to him that the wreckage was, in reality, a raft. Not much of a raft, he admitted, but it would serve its purpose. Once they were ashore, they could prop it up on two sticks so as to provide a temporary shelter. *After that.* He tried to stop the thought but it was no use. After that, they would abandon it.

He set himself to wait.

Determined not to die, he began to make plans for the trip ahead, reconstructing the shore in his mind. It would be a hard trip. There were rivers and swamps to cross but he knew where he was going and he was determined to get there. As he prepared for the struggle before them, he reached out, from time to time, to the right and left to reassure himself that Bob and Arni were still there and that their heads were out of the water. In turn, they did the same for him. Again and again, in the darkness they touched each other's faces as tenderly, as awkwardly as new lovers. Patiently, they waited for the dawn, certain that it would come and certain that the clouds would open like a vast curtain and the heavens give them a sign.

BEAR

"Bear again, Bodli," Monan David shouted through the screen door.

Bodli snatched the cast-iron frying pan off the stove. Shaking his fingers to cool them, he rushed outside.

He was about 50, with a long, heavy body and short, stumpy legs. When he hurried, he held his fists curled to his chest and waved his elbows so vigorously that he looked like a bird with clipped wings trying to fly. Because it was an unseasonably warm September morning, all that he was wearing was an old pair of black leather shoes, a white undershirt, and blue cotton pants held up by red braces. The skin on his chest and back was pale and puckered like crepe paper over which water had been sprinkled but his head, neck and lower arms were sunburned to a deep brown.

Half way across the lot, he passed Monan David. Helgi, his second hired man, was sitting on a fish box, his hands grasping his bony knees. "I can see it but I don't believe it," he said as Bodli came close enough to hear him.

What he was studying was the ice-house door. It slumped on one hinge. Lying on the ground was a two-by-four they had spiked across it the previous evening.

"That bloody devil!" Bodli exclaimed. "What's missing this time?" He was so wrought up that the words were choked out, thick and slow, like wood chips.

"Front quarter," Helgi answered. He reached out and ran a grimy finger over a bent spike.

Bodli clambered over the six-inch sill into the ice-house.

His shoes had no laces and to keep them from slipping off, he lifted his knees high and kept his toes angled sharply upward. The beef was gone. He could see that at a glance. He shivered and rubbed his shoulders briskly. Even with the door open, the ice-house was dark and close with the mouldy smell of old hay.

"Better leave well enough alone," Monan David warned, accurately reading his thoughts. "That new conservation officer won't like you shooting no bear in his territory."

Monan David was thin and small with a sly face and narrow, pointed chin. He looked like he should steal purses. When he talked to anyone, he always positioned himself so that he could look at them from the corners of his eyes. His grandmother, to celebrate his birth, had drunk a pint of homebrew and fallen asleep on a dirt road. A car had run over her ankles and the driver's insurance company had settled a small monthly payment on her. Since then, Monan David, because he was linked in her mind with prosperity, had been her favourite grandson. Despite their failings, the women in his family had a sense of both history and style and had named him Monan David III. Both his father and grandfather were called Joe.

"Okay," Bodli agreed, his thumbs hooked in his belt loops. "Since you're so worried about the bear, you feed it. Whatever it eats, I'll take out of your wages."

When he came back out, Monan David was sitting beside Helgi and they were both admiring the plank. He sighed. They had to be watched all the time for when they finished a job, they automatically sat down. It seemed to be a conditioned reflex. He slammed the door behind him. Its remaining hinge broke and, slowly, the door toppled forward.

Except for pulling his feet back six inches, Helgi never moved. He was tall and round-shouldered and had a long, angry red nose. When he worked, he moved so slowly that he might have been labouring under a hundred feet of water. Now, without getting up from the box on which he was sitting, he leaned forward, grasped the corner of the door that had come within inches of striking him and pulled it onto his lap. His philosophy of life, Bodli was sure, was don't stand if you can sit, don't sit if you can lie down, don't move if you can be still. He was, in all probability, one of God's mistakes and should have been a tree.

"Nail it back in place," Bodli ordered. "That ice melts and we can close down before we get properly started. As he watched, they fitted the door into place and propped the two-by-four against it. "We've got to do something about that bear." His voice was tinged with bitterness.

Monan David did not reply so Bodli went back to the kitchen and took two Tums. His hired men gave him a constant stomach ache. To get them to the camp on time, he had been forced to pay their fines for stealing a case of beer. Then, because their families had nothing, he advanced them money for rent and groceries. Before they started work, they had collected half their salaries. At the end of every season, he promised himself that he would leave them to their fate but during their absence he always envisioned them reforming and, as an act of faith, hired them back.

As he tried to make up his mind about the bear, he slid the frying pan onto the stove and sliced some cold potatoes into it.

He knew what bear it was. It was big, bigger than any he had seen in years. A white scar ran over the top of its head and angled across its face, giving it a particularly evil expression. Evidence of it had first appeared at the garbage dump. That had concerned him but it hadn't frightened him for it was far enough away not to be a problem. But then the bear had come to plague the camp. He thought of it as Helgi and Monan David's bear. To keep bears away, Bodli always took the fish offal two miles to the dump. Helgi had taken over the job but, out of laziness, he had gradually dumped the refuse closer and closer to the camp. Helgi, he told himself, was a damn fool. And what was worse, he was a bigger one for constantly giving him chances to redeem himself.

The front quarter had cost him $75 plus $5 for transportation. There was no regular freight and the foreman from the pulp camp down the road had brought it on the front seat of his car. When it came, it was wrapped in white muslin and the driver, because of the bad roads, had strapped it in place with the seat belt. Then he had hung his red toque over the end. The sight had given Bodli a momentary turn.

"You got a hammer?" Monan David asked from the doorway, simultaneously rising up on his toes to get a look at how breakfast was coming. All the time he was at home he never ate. His money went for vanilla extract. If the off-season had been any longer, he would have died from malnutrition. From the time he arrived at the camp, he gobbled anything edible with a voraciousness that was frightening. Bodli sometimes felt that if he didn't keep producing food, Monan David would consume everything, fish, furniture, equipment and, finally, when everything else was gone, him.

Bodli brought a hammer from his tool box. He had a blue scribbler in which he marked the date, time and borrower of any tool. When he was young, he had apprenticed as a carpenter and although he hadn't stayed long enough to get his journeyman's papers, he still treasured his tools and kept close track of them.

"You got another hinge?" This time it was Helgi. His eyes were fixed on the pan and his large Adam's apple jerked up and down inside the red, ridged tube of his throat.

Bodli would have liked one of them to do the cooking so he could fix the door but he knew that wouldn't work. Whichever one he chose would steal the food and trade it for liquor. As he dug out a hinge, he shook his head. They both needed a keeper, someone to constantly watch over them to save them from themselves. That was, in a way, what he did when he brought them north to where there was a clean, warm place to stay, decent meals and no liquor.

"Why me?" he said out loud. He had, over the years, grown used to talking to himself. "There are lots of other camps."

Much as he hated to admit it, Bodli knew Monan David and Helgi were right about the conservation officer. He was 25 and walked so stiffly that he gave the impression bending your knees was against departmental policy. He knew more about rules and regulations and less about the bush than anyone Bodli had ever met.

Even more serious to Bodli was his lack of a decent weapon. All he had was a single-barrel shotgun he had won in a poker game. He had two slugs and a box of shells loaded with buckshot. Except at point-blank range, the buckshot was no good. He wished he had a proper rifle. When he glanced out the window, his two hired men were sitting down, their attention alternately divided between the hinge and the door. He was sure they were hoping someone would come to finish the job for them. If someone had suddenly appeared to perform the task, Bodli would not have been surprised. It would just have been one more person from the Welfare Department. He snorted in disgust. When things went badly he didn't go whining for help. He did without.

"Hey, breakfast," he yelled through the screen door. They both shot to their feet. "As soon as you finish that job."

They were both seated at the table in ten minutes.

"What did you decide about the bear?" Helgi asked. His face drooped so much that invisible weights might have been hung from the corners of his mouth and eyes. Drunk or sober, he never smiled.

"We're going to shoot it."

Helgi rolled his eyes in disbelief but his square jaw never stopped its determined, rhythmical movement. His hands worked automatically, as if disconnected from the rest of his body, his knife labouring to push as much as possible onto his fork. After swallowing, he said, "Nowadays, that isn't the way to do it. You could get into a lot of trouble. It might be better just to put another plank over the door. Make a complaint and let the government handle it."

Each time Helgi took a mouthful of food, he thrust the

fork so far into his mouth that Bodli feared he would lose his grip on it and drop it straight into his stomach.

Bodli glowered at them but he knew that their knowledge of the government was inexhaustible. They were always dealing with it—welfare workers, police, probation officers, judges. It never ended. They never did anything for themselves, waiting passively, instead, for the government to decide what it should do for them. At the moment, they were less concerned about their wages than how soon they would have enough stamps in their unemployment books. They were times they acted as if they were mechanical appendages to some huge machine instead of human beings with wills of their own.

"We've got to get that bear," Bodli insisted. He refused to let them shake his faith. All that mattered finally was what you did for yourself. "I've got enough money for another quarter of beef and that's all. If we do nothing he'll take that too. Besides, if he's so bold, when he can't find anything in the ice house, he'll come into the bunkhouse. You might be sort of tough and strong tasting but he won't mind. Meat's meat."

He saw them glance apprehensively at each other. Even if nothing else interested them, their own survival did. A 400-pound bear rummaging through the camp every night looking for a free meal was not a situation even they could accept calmly. Bears, at the best of times, were bad tempered and unpredictable. One moment, they would be timid and easily frightened and the next moment they would turn and attack.

Watching Monan David and Helgi stuffing themselves, Bodli thought it might not be such a bad thing for them to be visited by a bear. Tribulation sometimes brought out unexpected qualities. At the very least, they might be startled into moving at a decent speed for once in their lives.

"We're going to take turns staying up tonight," he informed them in a voice that brooked no argument. "Whoever sees him can get me and I'll come with the shotgun."

Bodli left them repairing the bunkhouse roof and went to the garbage dump to collect a boxful of tin cans. Sitting spraddle-legged on the steps, he used a nail to punch two holes in each tin, then strung the tins on an old piece of sideline. When he was finished, he wove the cans across the door like a Christmas decoration. Satisfied, he stepped back, admired his work and, in a moment of pride, thumbed his braces until they hummed like banjo strings.

That evening, Helgi asked Bodli if he had fixed the radio. Bodli said he hadn't. Two days after they arrived, he had replaced a good tube with a burned-out one. Every night, when he was by himself, he put the good tube back so that he could listen to the news and weather, then he changed the tubes around again. He felt guilty for being so devious but he had no choice. It was standard practice for hired men to have an arrangement with their wives to put messages on CBC radio urgently requesting them to return home because there was an emergency. The only real emergency was that they were afraid of staying long enough to get used to working.

One wife had gone so far as to send a message saying that she was dying. It had worked so well the first time that she had sent similar messages every year. So far, she had been struck down by a heart attack, cancer, a stroke and diptheria. Everyone on the lake called her Dying Molly.

Personally, Bodli could not imagine why either Monan David or Helgi wanted to go home. He had seen what was on the other end.

Monan David's wife was four foot ten and so fat that her eyes were hidden in deep crevices. They were like little glistening, scurrying animals. Lizards, Bodli thought. The fatter she got, the less you could see of her eyes. Some day, he imagined, she would only be one potato chip away from blindness. Her black hair was chopped short and so frizzed that she might have curled it by sucking her fingers and sticking them into a wall socket. Where folds of flesh pressed against each other there were edges of grime. The only time she changed out of her pink housecoat was when she took a taxi to the liquor commission or went to bingo.

Bad as she was, she could have been chosen homemaker of the year next to Helgi's wife.

At two o'clock the next morning, Helgi woke Bodli. There had been no sign of the bear. Outside, there was a pale sliver of moon. The surface of the water was like washed slate. Trees and buildings had fused, become heavy and solid and seemed to have shrunk, as if the darkness, in some mysterious way, made everything smaller. As he gathered the thermos of coffee he had made for himself, his shotgun and his flashlight, he felt that every building was sealed inside a black chrysalis, without any cracks or ridges on which he could get a purchase. Sometimes, at night, when he was unable to sleep, he worried that death might be like that.

Outside, the air was damp and cold. He gave an involuntary shiver, pushed up his sheepskin collar, then sat with his back pressed to the bunkhouse wall. He had no intention of being surprised from behind. From where he sat, it was about a hundred feet down a steep, rocky slope to the icehouse door.

As he waited, he nervously fingered the shell in his left pocket, turning it end over end, feeling the ridged brass casing and smooth cardboard cylinder. He checked the safety. The gun had always jumped open when he fired it. The first time it had happened, the ejected shell had struck him in the eye and he thought he had been blinded.

To protect himself, he had fitted a band of copper wire over the barrel. Each time he fired the gun, he had to push the wire loop forward, break open the gun, load it and pull the loop back into place. He was reviewing the steps when he fell into a doze.

Tin cans rattling woke him. Startled, he jerked to his feet, dumping the flashlight from his lap. While he scrambled about, trying to find it, the tin cans continued to bang and clank. There was the soft, tearing sound of spikes being pulled out of dry wood. On his knees, he searched the slope until his hand closed over the flashlight. Grabbing it up, he clicked it on and stabbed the darkness with the light. A bear was standing on its hind legs, the claws of one foot dug into the two-by-four. Resting the shotgun along the flashlight, he took careful aim but Monan David came running around the corner and jostled him just as he fired.

The bear roared in pain, dropped to his front feet and rushed up the slope.

"Git, git," he heard Monan David shouting in a high, thin voice. Frantically, Bodli tried to shove down the copper wire and only succeeded in jamming it. He saw Monan David throw a stone, then heard him flee.

The door banged shut. With the bear looming massively before him, Bodli flung the shotgun into its face, then clambered up the ladder which had been left in place earlier in the day. At the foot of the ladder, the bear stopped. Bodli kicked the ladder over and crawled higher.

Sitting astride the peak of the roof, he pried a brick loose from the chimney and flung it down. The bear snarled and pawed at the building but Bodli knew he was safe.

He was tempted to stay on the roof. The bear and Helgi and Monan David were all below in the darkness and would have to decide their own fates. He leaned over and peered at the ground. For all he could see, he might as well have been on top of a mountain. Staying where he was, aloof from everything, was attractive, but he knew he could not remain. When he was sure the bear was gone, he reluctantly climbed down.

"Did you hit it?" Helgi asked excitedly as he peered from behind the half-opened door.

"I think so." When he found his shotgun, his hands were shaking so much that he couldn't open it.

To Bodli's dismay, there was a dark trail of blood. Instead of wounding the bear, he would rather have missed it altogether. Then he could have carefully planned their next confrontation. Now, he had no choice but to track it until he was sure it was dead.

"Gut shot," Monan David remarked, running his finger through the blood. "Best to leave him alone. He'll crawl into a hole and bleed to death."

There was no use trying to sleep, so they went to the kitchen for coffee. In half an hour, the sky started turning silver, then, in a while, a low, narrow bank of clouds turned red so that it stretched across the sky like a fresh wound. They watched the sun rise clear and yellow from the water.

"We should go see the conservation officer," Helgi suggested. "If he wants, he can get a helicopter and dogs and half the damn army."

Bodli shook his head. "We did it, we have to make it right." He held up the shotgun. Its stock was split. He loaded the gun with the second slug.

"Leave it be," Helgi insisted. He leaned forward. "If we don't say anything, nobody needs to know you shot it."

"It's Sunday. There'll be berry pickers on the road."

They looked outside. The cloud had disappeared and the sun was slowly rising into a clear sky. The day would be warm. Everyone who could, would be out enjoying the last pleasant days of fall.

At first, following the trail of bloodstains was easy for there was a lot of bare limestone. Bodli took the lead. Helgi came next. He had armed himself with a narrow triangular blade. As they picked their way along, the two hired men kept a nervous lookout on both sides.

Even at the brightest time of day the ground beneath the spruce forest was wound with shadow. The light that sifted down seemed to have been mixed with the grey dust that clung to the sloping branches. Underfoot, the thick layer of needles was the colour of rusted iron. As they walked, their feet made no sound.

Within a mile, they found where the bear had rested. The pale green moss was stained with dark blood and where the bear, in its pain, had churned convulsively at the ground, a hole had been torn in the soft, fleshy growth. A short distance farther, the blood, though less frequent, was fresher.

Here they hesitated, for the high ground gave way to a low, swampy area that had been burned over five years before. Among the charred tamarack trunks, which rose like thin fingers of black slag, there was a thick tangle of young willow, highbush cranberry and fireweed.

"I'm not going in there," Helgi protested with a shake of his head. "Not on your life." It was the first time one of them had spoken.

Bodli studied the bush for a sign of the bear. After the darkness under the spruce, the light was dazzling. He squinted and hooded his eyes with his left hand. Bodli wished it had been overcast. A cold, wet day would have eased the urgency by keeping the berry pickers, picnickers and fishermen off the road and beach.

"You don't want to come, go back," he replied, feigning indifference. "But this has got to be done."

The other two rotated as stiffly as tin figures in a pinball game, studying the forest around them. Grass and shrubs and shadows pressed close.

"What if he's near? What if he's circled around behind us?" Monan David whispered hoarsely. "Did you see his paw marks in that wet spot we crossed? They're bigger than my hand. What if we go out there? There isn't a tree big enough to climb and that bush'll get in the way if we try to run. You might as well try to escape in mud up to your knees."

Bodli watched them from half-closed eyes. He stood slumped, the shotgun cradled in his arm. "You think we could outrun him? Even if the ground was bare?"

No-one spoke. A single crow flew over and they followed it with their eyes until it was out of sight. Bodli had always admired the crows. Whatever they did was done for a purpose. They fended for themselves throughout the long winter. Their lives were ordered and deliberate.

"No," Helgi admitted at last. "There'd be no use. He'd run us down."

"If we don't get him, you know what'll happen?" Bodli

shifted the shotgun and his eyes searched the green plants that had sprung from the scorched earth. "He'll hunt you. He'll be behind every tree. When you open a door, he'll be behind that. Every time you go out at night, you'll hear him waiting. Every time you turn your back, you'll feel him breathing on your neck."

Bodli started away, following the bruised wake of their quarry. The other two, as if they were attached to him by strings, jerked to their feet and followed.

"It ain't right," Helgi cried softly in a desperate voice, his head turning from side to side.

Bodli was pressing forward, watching for danger from the corners of his eyes without ever letting his attention stray from the path he followed.

"This ain't fair," Monan David added. "Why didn't you leave us be? We was happy in jail. Nobody asked you to come and get us out."

Bodli walked stooped over, studying the ground, holding the shotgun close to his body. The stock was split. If it hadn't been for the butt plate, it would have fallen apart. The barrel was worn to a dull silver and, at some time, the bead had been knocked off.

"It's not much of a gun to risk our lives on," Helgi complained.

"All we can do is what we've got," Bodli answered without pausing.

Ahead, there was a flash of brown. Bodli jerked the gun to his shoulder but didn't shoot.

"What's the matter?" Monan David asked.

"Too far, too much brush between. We've got to get in close. All I've got is one slug."

Cautiously, they crept forward. Here, the trees clustered like black arrows in a quiver. The deadfall that littered the ground slowed them. Whenever they touched the shrivelled and eroded wood, charcoal stained their clothes and skin.

In the distance, they could hear cars. Now and again there were sharp, indefinite noises that might have been car doors slamming and women's and children's voices. A man's voice never carried far. Except for their own harsh breathing and the occasional snapping of a twig, they made no sound. Bodli's mouth was dry. He wished they had brought water. With every step the shotgun became heavier. Monan David was using the axe, head down, for a cane and Helgi dragged the ice chisel by the end.

Twice more they caught sight of the bear. It was slowing down and Bodli thought it was dragging one leg. Much as he wanted to, he refused to shoot until he was sure he couldn't miss. Wounding the bear again would only enrage it further and make it more dangerous.

On the edge of a clearing, they had to stop to catch their breath. The ground was still uneven and treacherous but Bodli studied the open area with relief. Here, the fire had been more intense, consuming nearly everything except for three trees directly ahead of them. The middle tree had, at its crown, two burnt stubs of branches so that it seemed to be topped by a small cross.

"Where do you think he is?" Helgi asked. He leaned on the steel bar. Its blade was over a foot long and tapered to a needle point.

"We'll just have to follow his tracks. He's wherever they stop."

When they touched the grass, crickets whirred briefly through the air but the grass, while still green, was stiff with fall. An occasional frog trilled. In the silence, the sound was dry and sudden.

In the centre of the ragged circle, the bear rested in a small hollow. Its breathing, like that of its pursuers, was laboured. Its right hind leg was stiff and, from time to time, it pulled at its wound. The bear was big but he was too thin for September. He should have been round and sleek. Instead, he was gaunt and his pale brown fur was dull. Too tired to run anymore, he lay, conserving his strength, listening to the rustling of the grass as he waited for a final confrontation. Just before him there was a fallen tree, its trunk still intact, and it formed a barrier about three feet from the ground. He waited until he saw the grass move in front of him, then sprang to his full height.

Too tired to go around, Bodli had decided to climb over the tree trunk. To do so safely he had raised the shotgun in his left hand and swung one leg over the trunk so that at the moment of the bear's attack he was off balance. When he saw the large head loom before him with its ragged scar and the one small, red pig-like eye and the other, white and blank as an egg, Bodli realized, with a sense of surprise, that he was going to die. Even so, he made a desperate attempt to bring the shotgun down and fire but the bear's right paw swept across the small space, its long, yellow nails disemboweling him and flinging him sideways.

The bear surged over the tree. Instead of attacking and giving Bodli a chance to crawl clear, Helgi dropped the chisel and ran. Monan David let out a low, pitiful cry, then followed. Bodli had jerked to his knees and with the shotgun held before him like a spear, thrust it toward the bear and pulled the trigger. The bear reeled away.

Bodli dropped the shotgun, laced his hands over his abdomen and knelt with one shoulder against the middle tree. He looked as if he were straining to lift a massive cross onto his shoulder. Blood ran over his fingers. In the distance, he heard someone beat on a car horn. He listened, as if expecting a message, but the sound stopped as abruptly as it had started.

"I'm coming," he said. But when he tried to move his knees, someone had sewn his legs to the ground. Neither Helgi nor Monan David was in sight.

Abruptly the ground tilted and he slipped sideways.

The one crow he had seen earlier returned, leading a flock of twenty or thirty others. When Bodli fell, he had rolled onto his back. One eye had slewed to the left, the other stared straight ahead, its pupil only a pin-prick but he knew the birds were there. They weren't flying with secret purpose as they usually did. Instead, they were circling around each other. Flapping their black wings, they climbed and fell erratically as they circled round and round without direction, filling the air with their bad-tempered, rasping voices.

Then, as the birds churned upward like dirty rags caught in a whirlwind, Bodli's eyes turned into their sockets. It was as if, unable to look upon a world he no longer could understand, he had chosen to explore the growing darkness within.

A BUSINESS RELATIONSHIP

Olga woke just before dawn. Even so, Carl was already up, huddled before the stove, his winter jacket pulled close around his shoulders. Although he was intent on splicing a broken cable, as soon as Olga entered, he looked up.

Ever since he had become sick, he had been unable to keep warm. His feet were constantly cold. Around the house, he wore two pairs of heavy wool socks inside his slippers. Lately, the growing pain had made him so restless that he was unable to sleep more than two or three hours at a time.

"I never heard you get up," she said. For the past week he had been sleeping on the chesterfield. Neither of them liked the arrangement but, more and more, the chores had become Olga's responsibility and they both knew that if she was going to do them herself, she needed to get her sleep.

"It's all right. I had some work to do."

"I'll make some fresh coffee," she offered, bustling forward and taking the pot from the stove. "That'll be bitter from standing all night. Would you like some cinnamon toast?"

He shook his head. He no longer ate or drank much except coffee.

Olga busied herself with her breakfast. She was a large, rawboned woman with a pink, hearty face and big hands and feet. She had a high forehead and a round chin that, like her cheeks, was always red. Carl had found her ten years before in the personal column of the Winnipeg *Free Press* where she was crammed into sixteen words—*Lady, 32, good character, cook, housekeeper, religious, wants to meet man of similar age. Object matrimony.*

Writing was difficult for Carl but he managed two short letters about himself. Then, the preliminaries over, he boarded the Saturday morning bus to Winnipeg. They met over a cup of tea in her landlady's shabby parlour. The air had been sour with stale grease and her landlady hid behind the door. Although they couldn't see her, her asthmatic breathing had rasped back and forth across their nervous conversation. Because Carl kept milk cows, he was only able to stay until shortly before departure time for the afternoon bus. The visit was unsatisfactory for both of them but it had to do. Before he left, they had reached an agreement. They both prided themselves on being practical and they both knew what to expect out of their relationship. They were not a couple of romantic teenagers. He was to provide her with a husband and home while she was to be a housekeeper and helpmate.

After the door closed behind him, the landlady, her back as round as a stone with age, her eyes that greedily consumed the scraps of other people's lives, came scampering in, her hands washing themselves with excitement.

"Are you taking him? He's not much to look at?" She skittered to one side, then the other in a dance of anticipation. Olga had carefully kept Carl's letters in her purse so they wouldn't be read while she was out.

"Yes," she answered abruptly. "I'll be leaving at the end of the month."

There were no children or relatives to explain to so they were married exactly two weeks later. She wore her good striped green dress and a large hat decorated with paper carnations. He wore his black suit, which smelled of mothballs and dust. The minister's wife and the janitor were their witnesses.

She brought her belongings with her in a suitcase and a cardboard box that had originally held 24 cans of Campbell's soup. While they waited for the evening bus, they ate bacon and eggs in the depot coffee shop. At Eddyville, the bus stopped in front of the drugstore. From there it was a mile to Carl's house. She was unused to the country and as they started off down the road she had become more and more afraid.

Although he had not been a large man even then, during the last few months he seemed to be constantly shrinking. Every morning, more bone showed. His loss of flesh was like a constant erosion around the roots of trees. His black hair had stiffened to the texture of dry grass. His eyes had begun to cloud, as if a thin layer of calcium was settling over them and his nose and mouth had grown more prominent.

While she ate, Carl worked the strands of wire together, joining the pieces so tightly that they would be inseparable. He could never stand to be idle and lately, as he had to give up more and more of the heavy work, he had taken to repairing small pieces of equipment.

The kitchen was just big enough for the two of them but it was bright and cheerful. When she had come, Carl was living in the kitchen and bedroom. She had opened the living- and dining-rooms and hadcleaned and arranged until she was satisfied. He had made no objection. She had painted the kitchen cupboards white and the walls light yellow. Around the edges of the cupboard, she had stencilled red poppies.

The house was a storey and a half with four concrete pillars holding up the porch roof. The pillars made the house feel permanent, as if it had been tightly screwed into the soil. To the south of the porch were the graves of Carl's parents. Set side by side, they were old graves, leveled, covered with grass, joined by a single headstone. Behind the headstone were purple and white lilacs. At first, she had been nervous about graves being so close but, after a while, she was glad they were there. Her own mother had disappeared during the Nazi occupation of Poland. She and her father had fled to Canada, living first in Halifax, then Toronto and Winnipeg. On a trip to Toronto to buy cloth for his tailor's shop, her father had died of a heart attack. She couldn't afford to have his body returned so he had been buried without anyone at his funeral. After that, she lived on what she earned from making alterations for a men's store.

Now, against all habit, she lingered over her breakfast, taking a second cup of coffee, which she didn't want. There was a sudden squeal from below, which she immediately identified as coming from the sump pump. In ten years, she had come to know the house and land so well that it was as if she had never lived anywhere else. Since she had married, she had never returned to Winnipeg, not even to visit.

The yellow house sitting on the curve, a spruce tree set at each side of the entrance to the driveway, the wild grass cropped to a lawn by their dozen sheep and seven cows, made up her entire life. Once or twice a month, they went together to Eddyville for bingo on a Wednesday. Saturdays, if they needed groceries, she walked into town to the Co-op. Sundays, they went to church.

Crowded between a dirt road and the lake, their half-mile of land was only a thousand feet wide at its widest point but it was big enough for them. Behind the house, there was a narrow path that angled down to the dock where a green skiff was moored.

"It may not be much," he had said when they first stood on the road together in the growing dusk, studying the fading house and barn and listening to the cattle moving softly along the fence, "but its *ours*." She never forgot that.

She knew nothing of the country but she learned as quickly as she could. From the moment she put her ad in the paper, she was determined to see that whoever agreed to have her would never have reason to regret his decision. Olga had added a dozen each of chickens and ducks and a brace of geese. Besides taking care of the house, she helped with the chores. She planted a vegetable garden, gradually expanding it each year until it provided them with vegetables and fruit from one year's end to the next. The year before last, they had a few dollars to spare and Carl had brought her marigolds and snapdragons to add to her border of wildflowers.

"You should let me take you to the hospital," she said quietly.

His eyes rested on her, then he went back to splicing the cable, his thin hands moving with practised familiarity.

"We've got $2000. Do you know what a day in the hospital costs? $50, maybe $75. And then there's the doctor and the medicine." He said it evenly, without rancour or bitterness but with a puzzled tone as if unable to understand how lying in bed could cost so much.

She knew there was no use trying to explain. Like most people who work hard for everything, he was careful with his money. She didn't blame him. For $10 worth of fish, he had often gone out at dawn and stood all morning in a lurching, choppy sea, pulling nets from the bitter water. When he came back, he returned to farm chores that lasted into the evening.

"Everything is in your name. The $2000 is in the metal foot-locker." They had been over it all before but she listened without reminding him. "The title to the farm is in my top drawer and the money to pay the taxes." He paused, thinking ahead. "The worst will be when the cows are calving. You won't get much rest. Maybe," he added, momentarily unsure of himself, "you'll not want to stay by yourself. There are a lot of heavy chores."

"I should feed the cows," she answered but she didn't move.

"You can't do all the work and look after me at the same time."

She, like him, was a realist. She knew her own limits. "Yes," she agreed, "I can't do both."

"The black cow always has trouble with its calf. The vet from Eddyville will cost a few dollars but you'll need him."

"What about the boats and nets?"

As he considered the question, he sat with his mouth

pursed. "Sell them. You won't use them and every season they sit, they lose value."

She knew he was right but she wished she could have kept the boat. Sometimes, in nice weather, she had gone with him to his nets and they had eaten lunch together. Rocking gently on a vast silver plain, they seemed, at those times, to be the only two people on earth.

"I'll put up a sign in the Co-op store and the skating rink."

He nodded with approval.

She knew he was worried about money and she wanted him not to worry so she said, "If I need more, I can get a job cleaning the school or the bank. It isn't hard work and it only takes a couple of hours a day."

"Good." He nodded his head with approval. "They aren't the best jobs but you have to be practical."

They both liked to be practical but sometimes it was difficult. During Olga's first week on the farm, a woman had come to the door with chickens for $1.50 each. She had thought they were a wonderful bargain and bought four. She had roasted one for their supper but when she tried to cut it, the knife slid off the breast. Carl had managed to hack off a piece but no amount of chewing would soften it. They had eaten left-over cabbage rolls for supper. The next day, she had stewed the chicken for eight hours.

From time to time, Carl had come to ask if the chicken was cooked. His asking made her feel terrible but then she realized he was teasing and they had started to laugh. Ever since then, it had been their own private joke. Whenever she cooked chicken, he would ask if she was sure that it was ready and prod it gently with a fork before carving it.

"Maybe you will prefer to go back to the city," he said. "It will be lonely."

She thought about the sad, grey room that had made her desperate enough to advertise in the paper, desperate enough to expose herself to the ridicule of the world, and wished she had some way to explain what it meant to have her own pots and pans, her own kitchen, her own husband. Having always had a place of his own, he could not, she knew, ever really understand what it had been like to have to live in other people's rooms.

After a while she replied, "I'd rather be here. There are the animals and the garden. Eddyville is close enough for me to walk. If the roads are muddy, I can take the tractor."

They fell silent again, then more to himself than her, he said, "Jimmy, the Englishman, you know, the one I've told you about. He lived beside where I pull up my boat for the winter. He got sick and before it was finished, everything was gone. His wife had to live on welfare."

He had finished the cable. He pulled it tight, inspecting it to see that there were no loose strands. Satisfied, he coiled it and carefully put it in a box at his feet. She liked the fact that he was tidy and picked up after himself.

"The garden was good this year," he remarked. "You've learned to make a good garden. No-one would ever know you hadn't come from the country."

She flushed with pride.

He lifted himself up from the seat of his chair with one hand and craned to look out the window. He was not a carpenter but when she had mentioned that she would like to be able to look out as she worked at the counter, he had put in a window right away.

"It's really nice to have that window," she said. "The light is good for working."

He ducked his head, the way he did when he was embarrassed. "You need to feed the cows. They can't wait any longer."

She got up and put her mug in the sink.

"I'm going," he informed her, "to the marsh for some hay." He pulled on his rubber boots then, as if it was an afterthought, added, "I'll see if I can shoot a mallard for tomorrow's supper. If I'm a little bit late, don't worry."

"I won't," she lied. "Are you going right away?"

He took the shotgun out of the cupboard and stuffed a handful of shells into his pocket.

"Yes. It's already late." He hesitated at the door and she thought he was going to say something more but then he quickly went out. The tractor started with a roar. When she looked, he was turning out of the yard. She watched until he jolted out of sight behind a thicket of leafless poplar.

She went outside and saw that both pitchforks were leaning against the fence. The sky was clear and the air brisk. The blue dome of the sky went on forever. She thought that this was wrong, that it should have been grey and cloudy with a cold drizzle. The sun was too bright to look at directly so she stood watching it from an angle, wishing she could reach up and hold it in place with her bare hands, but then she heard the cows shuffling impatiently in the barn and, since there was no-one else to do the work, she went to pitch them hay from the loft.

Copyright © 1975 by W. D. Valgardson

All rights reserved: no part of this book may be reproduced in any form or by any means, electronic or mechanical, except by a reviewer, who may quote brief passages in a review to be printed in a newspaper or magazine or broadcast on radio or television.

Library of Congress Catalogue Card No. 74-31955

ISBN 0 88750 148 6 (hardcover)
ISBN 0 88750 149 4 (softcover)

Designed and edited by Michael Macklem

Printed in Canada

PUBLISHED IN CANADA BY OBERON PRESS

AUG -8 1983